"I won't be your mistress."

He too shot out of his chair. "I'm not looking for a mistress."

"Good, because I won't be one. Not ever. I learned all I wanted to know about having uncommitted sex with a guy so primitive he should be in a museum. The next time I have sex with a man I'm going to have a ring on my finger and an avowal of love to go with it!"

"Just who is this man?" he demanded in a near roar.

"I don't know, but when I find him he won't be anything like you!"

"You think not?" Then he reached out, yanking her to him. "I think this mythical man will be just like me because he will be me. No other man touches the mother of my child."

He'd said the words a breath above her lips and then closed the distance. And the electric current of desire was there, waiting, lurking in her deepest subconscious to come to the fore with the first touch of his mouth to hers.

Lucy Monroe started reading at age four. After she'd gone through the children's books at home, her mother caught her reading adult novels pilfered from the higher shelves on the bookcase…alas, it was nine years before she got her hands on a Mills & Boon® romance her older sister had brought home. She loves to create the strong alpha males and independent women that people Mills & Boon® books. When she's not immersed in a romance novel (whether reading or writing it) she enjoys travel with her family, having tea with the neighbours, gardening and visits from her numerous nieces and nephews. **Lucy loves to hear from readers:** e-mail LucyMonroe@LucyMonroe.com, visit www.LucyMonroe.com, or write to 1401 Marvin RD NE #307, PMB 275, Lacey, WA 98516, USA.

Recent title by the same author:

THE GREEK TYCOON'S ULTIMATUM

THE BILLIONAIRE'S PREGNANT MISTRESS

BY
LUCY MONROE

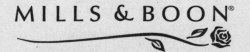

MILLS & BOON®

To my Resident Alpha Male
You are and will always be the hero of my heart.
Thank you for believing in me. I love you.

*First published in Great Britain 2003
Harlequin Mills & Boon Limited,
Eton House, 18-24 Paradise Road, Richmond, Surrey TW9 1SR*

© Lucy Monroe 2003

ISBN 0 263 83343 7

*Set in Times Roman 10½ on 12 pt.
01-1203-45944*

*Printed and bound in Spain
by Litografia Rosés, S.A., Barcelona*

PROLOGUE

THE cold porcelain of the bathroom sink pressed against Alexandra Dupree's forehead as she leaned against it, her stomach still heaving from its third early-morning upset in as many days. She dragged air into lungs starved by the unpleasant moments spent bent over the sink.

After a minute of doing nothing but breathe, she tentatively brought her body erect. A small twinge of nausea hit her, but she was able to control it. Okay, as unpleasant as this new early morning ritual had become, she had something even less pleasant to perform. She stared at the small white stick with all the wariness she would feel for a snake found curled around the base of the commode.

Dimitri had been fanatical about using birth control. So she'd convinced herself one late period didn't mean anything, until she woke up heaving three days ago. At first she'd thought she had the flu, sure there could be no possibility she was pregnant even though the condom had broken a month ago. Her menses had come right on time a week later.

She still didn't understand how this could be possible, but she had too many symptoms to deny. Her breasts were tender. She was tired all the time. She'd cried when Dimitri told her he had to spend more time in Greece and wouldn't be returning to their Paris apartment for several days. She never cried.

She forced herself to do what was necessary for the pregnancy test. Ten minutes later the world went white

5

around the edges as she stared at the blue line confirming she carried the child of Dimitrius Petronides.

Dimitri clenched his fists, refusing to give vent to his frustration.

"You know it is time. You are thirty, heh? You need a wife, some babies, a home." The older man's gray head tilted arrogantly, while he fixed Dimitri with a look that said he would argue this to the ground.

Dimitri had no desire to argue anything with his grandfather. He had barely survived a heart attack five days ago. Dimitri smiled. "I'm hardly in my dotage, Grandfather."

The man who had raised Dimitri and his brother since their parents' deaths snorted. "Don't try to get around me with your charm. It won't work. You're my heir and I need to go to my grave knowing you will do your duty by the Petronides name."

Dimitri's heart contracted. "You are not going to die."

His grandfather shrugged. "Who of us is to say when we will die? But I'm old, Dimitrius. My heart is not as strong as it once was. Is it so much to ask you marry Phoebe now? Why put it off? She's a sweet girl. She'll make you a proper Greek wife. She'll give you Petronides babies."

Eyes sliding shut, the older man breathed shallowly as if his short speech had taken more out of his weakened physical state than he had to give. Dimitri wanted to do something, but he was powerless. His grandfather's doctors wanted the old man to have heart surgery, but he had refused to discuss it.

"Why won't you have the by-pass operation your doctor is recommending?"

"Why won't you marry?" the old man countered. "Perhaps if I had great-grandchildren to look forward to, the pain of such an operation would be worth going through."

Dimitri felt the blood drain from his face. "Are you saying you won't have the operation if I don't marry Phoebe Leonides?"

Dark blue eyes, so much like his own, opened to stare at Dimitri with all the stubbornness a Petronides male had to bear. "Yes."

CHAPTER ONE

ALEXANDRA nervously smoothed the kerchief style silk halter-top over the nonexistent bump where her baby rested under her heart.

The unaccustomed warmth of late spring had allowed her to wear the sexy outfit to boost her flagging morale. She turned to the side and surveyed herself in the full-length mirror in her bedroom. Her willowy body encased in the champagne silk hip-hugging pants and sexy halter looked no different than it had when Dimitri had left for Greece.

The week-old knowledge that she was pregnant with his child might show in her wary hazel eyes, tinted sultry green by colored contacts, but it had not yet affected the shape of her body. She adjusted the gold chain belt resting low on her hips and the multiple thin bangles she wore on her wrist tinkled like small bells as they clinked together. Then in a nervous gesture, she pulled another curling strand of her hair down to frame the soft angles of her face.

Curled and professionally bleached so many shades, it looked like rippling sunlight when she let it down, her hair was a Xandra trademark. Only right now, she didn't feel like Xandra Fortune, popular model and lover to Greek Tycoon, Dimitrius Petronides. She felt like Alexandra Dupree, daughter of an old New Orleans family, convent educated and shocked to be unmarried and pregnant with her lover's child.

"You look beautiful, *pethi mou*."

Alexandra spun away from the mirror. Dimitri stood in the door, masculine appreciation burning in his startling blue eyes. For a moment she forgot her condition. Forgot the many truths she needed to tell him. Forgot her fears. Forgot everything but how much she had missed this man over the past three weeks.

She flew across the room and threw herself against his chest. "*Mon cher*, I have counted the minutes since you left!"

Strong arms locked around her in an almost convulsive movement while his body remained strangely stiff. "It has only been a month and you have been busy with work. You cannot have missed me that much."

His words reminded her how he had resented her refusal to quit modeling when they had become lovers, but she had not wanted to be any man's kept mistress. Nor had she had the option of quitting her job. She needed the money she made to support the family he knew nothing about.

"You are wrong. Nothing can keep me so occupied I do not notice your absence. A day. A week. A month. I grieve them all." She grimaced inwardly at her blatant vulnerability. Where had her sophisticated cool gone, the career model facade that had initially drawn Dimitri to her?

The first crack had appeared when he'd told her he was going to be in Greece longer than anticipated and she'd cried. After two-and-a-half weeks of morning sickness, a positive pregnancy test and her mother's horrified reaction to the news, the Xandra Fortune persona was in definite risk of extinction.

*   *   *

Dimitri tried to hold on to his self-control, not an easy thing around Xandra. And this was Xandra as he'd never seen her. Clingy. Almost vulnerable, but he knew that could not be true. They had become lovers a year ago and although she shared her body with a generosity that moved him, she kept her heart and parts of her life hidden from him.

Their relationship was modern and free of long-term commitment, something she'd made it clear by her actions she did not expect from him.

She pressed her body to his in blatant invitation and he laughed. "You mean you have grieved my absence from your bed, do you not?"

That was the only place he was convinced she did need him. She wouldn't let him support her, making it obvious she would rather spend time away from him than give up any part of her career. None of this, however, made it easier to say what needed to be said. In fact, he was sure it would be harder for him to say the words than for her to hear them. His sophisticated lover would not appreciate a drawn out, or emotional goodbye any more than he would.

She shook her head, stretching up to link her hands behind his neck and brushed the hair at his nape. "I missed *you*, Dimitri. There was no joy in cooking for myself alone, no pleasure in watching the French Open without you to mutter when your favorite double-faulted on game point."

He frowned, remembering the play. She smiled at him with a look that spelled his doom if he didn't get his news out quickly. It had already wrought an instant response in his body. "I have news I must tell you."

Her arms went stiff in reaction to the seriousness of his tone. "Can it not wait, *mon cher?*"

He reached behind his neck to remove her hands, but she locked her fingers with surprising force.

He clasped her wrists. "We must talk now."

Alexandra did not want to talk. She was not ready to share her news. He'd seduced her from the beginning. She'd given him her heart, her body and her fidelity, as committed to him as any wife could be. Only she wasn't his wife and she didn't know how he'd respond to his lover getting pregnant.

Fear more than desire prompted her hips to grind against him. "No." She kissed his chin, tasting the skin and letting her body absorb the return of its other half. "No talk." She brushed her unfettered breasts behind her thin top back and forth across the crisp white silk of his shirt. "First, this."

"Xandra, no." He pulled her hands away from his neck, but made the mistake of letting them go.

She tunneled under his jacket and pushed it off his shoulders. "Dimitri, yes."

He glared at her, but he did not stop her from pushing his suit coat to a pile of expensive Italian designer fabric on the floor. She smiled in approval. "I want you, Dimitri. We can talk later."

She needed the affirmation that they were two halves of the same whole before she could tell him the truth about the baby she carried and equally as terrifying, the truth about who and what she was.

He grabbed her round the waist and lifted her until her mouth was even with his own. "Heaven help me, I want you, too."

There was something about the angry tone in his voice she did not understand, but she could not focus on it for long, not with his warm lips closing over her own in overwhelming passion.

She tore at his tie while he made quick work of the two hooks holding her top together. He helped her with the buttons on his shirt. The two garments fell to the thick pile carpet together and his lips never separated from hers. He pulled her flush against his body and the naked flesh of her already aroused nipples brushed the heat of his muscular chest.

She shivered in reaction while he groaned.

"We should not be doing this."

The words registered only subliminally, planting a question as to why they should be said, but she could not consciously respond to them. She was too over-whelmed by the feel of his flesh against her own for the first time in over a month. He seemed similarly affected as his arms tightened around her until she could barely take a breath.

Seconds later they lay entwined on the bed, the rest of their clothes discarded, hungry hands touching inti-mate places, mouths devouring one another. They climbed to the heights together with a speed they never had before. When they tumbled into starbursts and obliv-ion, masculine shouts mingled with her own cries of pleasure.

Alexandra laid her hand over Dimitri's heart. It still beat with the accelerated pulse of recently spent passion.

"Such a strong heart," she murmured, "such a strong man." Would the news she had to share direct that strength toward her or against her?

His body tensed as if he had some premonition of what was to come. He rolled away and ejected himself from the bed. "I need a shower."

She stared at the six-foot-four-inch sexy giant tower-ing above the bed. Tension was emanating off him in waves.

"I'll join you."

He shook his head. "Stay there. I will be quick."

Her heart squeezed at the small rejection, but she smiled and nodded. "All right." Craven coward that she was, she gladly accepted another excuse to put off telling him her news.

He came out of the bathroom fifteen minutes later dressed in his usual sartorial elegance, but his dark hair was still damp. His choice of another business suit over something less formal made her pause.

"Do you have a meeting?"

The chiseled features of his gorgeous face were set in an unemotional mask. "Xandra, there is something I must tell you."

She scooted into a sitting position, pulling the sheet with her to shield her body from the blue gaze that had mesmerized her from the moment they met. "What?"

"I'm getting married."

Everything inside her went still. Had he said what she thought he had said? No. It wasn't possible. "M-married?"

His hands fisted at his sides, his body stiff with tension she could no longer ignore. "Yes."

She could not take it in. It had to be some kind of joke. "If this is your idea of a marriage proposal, you've got a lot to learn."

Sensual lips twisted in a grimace. "Do not be ridiculous."

"Ridiculous?" She wished her brain would start working again, but she couldn't think in the face of his words.

"You are a career woman as you've shown time and again over the past year." He slashed the air with one cutting hand. "A woman with your ambitions would not make a proper wife for the heir to the Petronides empire."

She shivered with a chill that went clear to the marrow of her bones. "What exactly are you saying?"

"I am getting married and naturally our liaison must come to an end." The sick paleness of his features did nothing to alleviate her personal pain.

"You told me our relationship was exclusive. You told me I could trust you. You would not make love to another woman while I shared your bed." She jumped out of that bed, feeling dirty and used, the passion they had shared soiled with his revelation.

Running his long fingers through the black silk of his hair, he sighed. "I have not had sex with another woman."

"Then who are you marrying?" she practically shrieked.

"No one you know."

"Obviously." Alexandra glared at him, wanting to kill him, wanting to scream, very afraid she would cry.

He sighed again. "Her name is Phoebe Leonides."

Greek. The other woman was Greek and probably meek, proper and brought up to marry money. "When did you meet her?" Though the pain was tearing her apart, she had to know.

"I've known Phoebe most of my life. She is the daughter of a family friend."

"You've known her most of your life and you just decided you loved her?"

A cynical laugh erupted from him. "Love has nothing to do with it."

He said love like it was a dirty word. Neither of them had ever spoken of love, but she adored Dimitri with every fiber of her being and had hoped that he had returned those feelings at least in some small way. Enough to make a marriage and family between them work now that she was pregnant with his child, but he quite obviously didn't believe in the emotion.

"If you don't love this woman, why are you marrying her?"

"It is time."

She swallowed convulsively. "You say that like it's something you'd always planned to do."

"It is."

Blood roared to her head, making her feel flushed and weak. She swayed.

He said something vicious in Greek and grabbed her upper arms to steady her. "Are you all right, *pethi mou?*"

What planet was he from? How could she be all right? He'd just told her he planned to marry another woman, a woman he'd always intended to make his wife while he'd spent the past year using Alexandra as his whore.

"Let. Me. Go," she got out between clenched teeth.

He dropped his hands, his face registering affront and she wanted to slap him so much it was an ache in her muscles. He took a single step back.

She glared up at the face that had been more beloved than any other since they met fourteen months ago. "Let me get this straight. You always planned to marry another woman?"

Indigo eyes narrowed. He didn't like repeating himself. "Yes."

"Yet you seduced me into your bed. You made me your tart knowing you never intended our relationship to be anything more than sexual?"

He reared back as if she'd struck him. "I did not make you my tart. You are my lover."

"Ex-lover."

His jaw clenched. "Ex-lover."

"Why…" She swallowed the bile rising in her throat. She couldn't ask this, but she had to. "Why did you make love, I mean…*have sex* with me just now?"

He spun away from her, his magnificent body sending messages to her own even amidst the carnage of their discussion.

"I couldn't help myself."

She believed him. She hadn't been able to help herself with him from the very beginning. She'd still been a virgin at the ripe age of twenty-two, but her innocence had been no barrier to the feelings he ignited in her.

He'd been shocked by her virginity, but not deterred in his resolve to make her his lover. She'd loved him and after two months of holding him off, she'd given in. It had been fantastic. He had made her feel cherished and there had been times over the past year when she had even felt loved.

"I don't believe you want to let me go." He couldn't.

"It is time," he said again, as if that explained it all.

"Time to marry the woman you intended to marry all along?" she asked, needing to make it very clear in her own mind.

"Yes."

Suddenly she felt her nakedness even through the mists of her anger and it shamed her. She had shared her body without inhibitions with this man for a year… a year during which he knew he planned to marry another woman.

She spun on her heel and headed to the bathroom where she jerked on the toweling robe she kept hanging on the back of the door. When she came back into the bedroom, Dimitri was gone. A search of the apartment revealed he had not merely left the bedroom, he had left her.

She stood in the middle of the living room and let the emptiness of the apartment sink into her consciousness until it was so heavy it forced her to her knees. Her head dropped, feeling too heavy for her neck and the sting of tears began in the back of her throat.

Soon their acid heat burned their way down her cheeks and neck to soak into the lapel of the heavy Turkish robe.

Dimitri was gone.

Dimitri leaned against the wall in the hallway outside the apartment. He'd forced himself to leave when Xandra went into the bathroom. If he hadn't, he would never have made it out the door. Even now, the temptation to go back to her and tell her it was all a mistake rode him hard.

But it was not a mistake. If Dimitri did not marry Phoebe Leonides, an old man whom Dimitri loved more than his own life or personal happiness, would die. His grandfather had refused to back down from his ultimatum and even now sat weakly in a wheelchair, refusing necessary surgery until Dimitri set a wedding date.

His fist jabbed viciously into the palm of his other hand. Why had Xandra mentioned marriage between them? Why taunt him with the impossible? She did not want marriage. She could not. If she had, at least one time over the past year, her career would have come second and he would have come first. It never had. Not once.

Xandra was angry right now, her feminine pride bruised. It had upset her to realize he had planned to marry another woman all along, but he could not take seriously the idea she thought their liaison would end in marriage. She'd made her independence too much an issue for that. However, she had obviously believed he had no plans at all in that direction.

More guilt added to the already swirling cauldron of emotions inside him.

He had not intended to make love with her again, but he'd lost his cool and his control the moment she went into seductive mode. For all her worldly sophistication, Xandra was not an aggressive lover. She was affectionate and responsive, more responsive than any woman he'd ever known, but she initiated lovemaking rarely and even then, she did so subtly. Her seduction just now had been anything but subtle and it had undermined his defenses with the impact of an invading army.

Afterward, it had been harder than he thought possible to tell her of his upcoming marriage while her body remained warm and fragrant from their intimacy.

He forced himself away from the wall and toward the elevator. A clean break was the only way.

Alexandra waited thirty-six hours to call Dimitri's cell phone, sure with the passing of each hour, the man she loved, the father of her child, would come back to her.

He had made love to her. She was sure he hadn't planned to do it, but he had. He'd never slept with Phoebe. He had said he didn't love the other woman and equally important, he couldn't possibly need her the way he had needed Alexandra for the past year.

But he did not come and she had no choice but to contact him. She was furious with him, more hurt than she'd ever been in her life, but she carried his child and she had to tell him before he made the mistake of marrying another woman.

She refused to consider what she would do if the news of impending fatherhood had no effect on his marital plans.

The sound of the phone ringing beeped in her ear three times before he picked up. "Dimitri, here."

"It's Xandra."

She was met with unnerving silence.

"We need to talk."

More silence. "There is no more to say."

"You're wrong. There are things I must tell you." Did he notice how alike her words now to the ones he'd spoken to her two days ago?

"Can we not dismiss the postmortems?"

She sucked in air, but controlled the desire to scream like a fishwife at the insensitive tycoon dismissing her like yesterday's garbage. "No. We need to talk. *You owe this to me, Dimitri.*"

This time she didn't break the silence.

Finally she heard a heavy exhalation at the other end of the line. "Fine. Meet me at *Chez Renée* for lunch."

"I'd rather meet in the apartment." She did not want to tell him of his impending fatherhood and her true identity in a public setting.

"No."

She gritted her teeth, but didn't argue. "Fine." Maybe a public setting would be best after all. *He would hesitate to commit murder with witnesses*, she thought with black humor.

They set a time and hung up.

Dimitri cut the cell connection and turned to look out the large window in his Athens office. He had flown to Athens within hours of leaving the Paris apartment. He hadn't trusted himself to stay in France and not go back to her.

And that infuriated him.

His grandfather's life was at stake and Dimitri refused to allow an obsession with a woman deter him from his purpose. His parents had taught him all the lessons he needed to learn in that area. His father's obsessive need for his mother had resulted in years of volatile togetherness and ultimately both their deaths.

He could not allow a similar compulsive need for Xandra to affect the same result for his grandfather.

He'd been her first lover, but with a sensual nature like hers, he knew he would not be her last. There had even been times when he wondered if he were her only lover. There were areas of her life she kept hidden from him. She took trips abroad that were not modeling assignments, but that she refused to discuss with him.

He had told himself he was being foolish. She did not flirt or make meaningful eye contact with other men. She had always been gratifyingly hungry when they came together, but he'd never been able to dismiss the feeling she did not belong exclusively to him. If not sexually, than emotionally.

Which had led him to believe she would take their eventual but inevitable breakup with her usual cool sophistication, just as she took their many separations made necessary by her work or his. A memory of her tear-clogged voice the last time he'd called to say his stay in Greece had been prolonged rose up.

What if she had convinced herself she loved him? He shuddered at the thought. Love was an excuse women used to succumb to their passions. His mother had supposedly loved his father, but she'd also loved her tennis instructor and then the husband of a business acquaintance and finally the Italian ski instructor she'd run off with.

His mother had been a prime example of the treachery women perpetrated in the name of love. Dimitri preferred the frank exchange of sexual desire to protestations of a fleeting emotion that only caused pain in the end.

But Alexandra wanted to meet one more time. His curled fist settled against the windowsill.

He'd agreed because she was right...he did owe her.

They'd spent a year together and she had given him the gift of her innocence. She'd made little of it at the time, but his traditional Greek upbringing had planted it as a debt firmly in his mind. A debt he should not have repaid with such a soulless dismissal of their relationship.

He hadn't even given her a gift in parting. She deserved better than that. She had been his woman for a year. He would make sure she was set for the future.

He could only hope his control at their upcoming meeting exceeded that of the last one.

CHAPTER TWO

ALEXANDRA remained seated while she waited for Dimitri to weave his way between the small bistro tables and join her. She'd chosen to sit outside, hoping the late spring sunshine would imbue their encounter with some much needed optimism. Dimitri's aviator sunglasses hid his expression from her, but his mouth was set in a grim line that did not bode well for the meeting ahead.

She resisted the urge to rub her temples, giving away the anxiety she felt.

He pulled out a chair opposite her own and folded his tall frame into it. "Xandra."

What a cold greeting for the woman he had been living with for the past year. She pulled the cloak of sophistication she wore like a protective covering around her and inclined her head. "Dimitri."

He pulled off the aviators and tossed them on the table. His blue eyes revealed no more of his thoughts than the mirrored reflection of his glasses had. "Have you ordered?"

Why that question should cause pain to slice through her, she had no idea. Perhaps because it exemplified a new level of distance between the two of them. He had not asked how she was or how her morning had gone. Presumably those topics were no longer of concern to him.

"Yes. I ordered you a steak and salad."

"Fine. I presume you have a specific reason for insisting we meet." As if the dissolution of their year long

22

relationship wasn't enough. "There is something I forgot to do at our last meeting as well." He grimaced. "It did not go as I expected."

She had thought she couldn't hurt more than she already did, but she had been wrong. Not go as he expected? They'd made love with desperate passion and then he'd ditched her. Which part hadn't he expected?

"There's something you need to know. Something I have to tell you before you..." She could not make herself say it.

His brow rose in query and he pulled a sheaf of papers from his briefcase. He laid them on the table and then placed a small box on top of them, a box obviously the size of a jewelry case. There was an attitude of finality in the action that cut the thread holding her composure.

"You can't marry her!" The words burst from Alexandra without thought. "She doesn't care about you. She couldn't and still accept your lifestyle for the past year."

Again that mocking black brow rose.

She answered the unspoken question. "You've been living with me." Surely no woman could tolerate such a circumstance and care even the least little bit for the man involved.

"I assure you, I have not publicized the fact."

She clenched her hand against her stomach, feeling as if she'd sustained a blow there.

He was right. He had been very careful to keep their relationship out of the media, no small feat when she was a fairly well known model in Europe and he was a billionaire. But those same billions along with her circumspect behavior had made it possible. She had her own reason for wanting to stay out of the international scandal rags.

Just as she'd had her reasons for keeping her identity as Alexandra Dupree a secret. Just as she had commitments that had forced her to put her job before her time with Dimitri. But those commitments no longer held top place in her priorities, not now that she was pregnant and he was talking about marrying another woman.

"Do you love her?" He'd implied he didn't, but she wanted facts. She needed assurances.

"Love is not something I think about."

That was telling her. She bit her lip, tasting blood before she realized what she was doing.

He swore and dipped his napkin in her glass of water before pressing it against the small wound, his expression furious. "Do not do this to yourself, Xandra. Our affair was bound to end. Perhaps that end is coming sooner than either of us expected or wanted, but it cannot be a complete shock to you."

She shook her head, unable to believe he thought she had spent the last year looking ahead to an end in their relationship. She had never allowed herself to imagine a future *with* him, either. In fact, she'd spent the last year pretty much refusing to think of the future at all.

"I love you." The words just slipped out.

"Damn it. Don't do this."

"Don't do what? Tell you the truth?"

"Try to manipulate me with such claims."

"I'm not trying to manipulate you."

Cynicism colored his features. "Then why have you said nothing of this great love for the past year?"

"I was afraid…"

His sarcastic laugh cut into her. "You were more sincere."

On one level, she understood his disbelief. She'd never spoken of love and he didn't know about Mama or Madeleine and the financial needs that had forced Alexandra to put him second to her modeling career. She might never have told him of her love either, but her pregnancy had forced her to reevaluate her life, a big chunk of which was her relationship with him.

Even understanding it, his scathing denial of her love still hurt. "You care about me. Don't try to deny it. Not after the way we have been the past twelve months, not after making love to me two days ago."

"I appreciate that having sex with you in the circumstances was wrong, but as I said I could not help myself."

Okay, so he hadn't agreed he cared about her, but such an admission from a guy like Dimitri Petronides wasn't something to dismiss lightly. He found her irresistible. Surely that must mean he had some feelings for her. "If it were only sex, you could have gotten that anywhere, including from your fiancée."

"A proper Greek girl does not give her innocence to a man before she marries."

Did he realize what he was saying? It was archaic. Prehistoric. "What does that make me? A tart?"

His broad shoulders tensed. "No. You are an independent, career-minded woman. I wanted you. You wanted me. We made no promises to one another. I never intended marriage and if you are honest with yourself you will admit you knew that."

"Why should I?" Maybe she hadn't thought ahead to marriage, but she sure as heck hadn't assumed they'd break up like this either. Not with him planning to marry someone else. "We had something incredibly special."

"We had great sex."

Her hands trembled and she put down the glass of

juice she had just lifted to her lips. "I can't believe you just said that."

"It is the truth."

"Your truth."

He shrugged. "My truth."

"Well, I have a truth I have to share with you as well."

"What is this truth?" he asked coolly.

It was hard, harder than she could ever have imagined to pluck up the courage to tell a man who had just informed her what she had mistaken for love had been nothing more than great sex that she carried his child. In the end only blunt honesty would do. "I'm pregnant."

For several seconds his expression did not change and then his eyes filled with pity. "Xandra, do not humiliate yourself this way. I will not leave you unprovided for."

He thought she was worried about the payoff gift? She glared at the pile of papers and jeweler's box near his right hand, wishing she could incinerate them with her eyes. "I'm carrying your child, Dimitri."

He groaned and rubbed between his eyes with his thumb and forefinger. "You've always been very forthright, very honest. Do not stoop to telling tales now. Surely you cannot believe it will change the outcome."

He thought she was lying? She felt hysterical laughter well up inside her. He thought she was lying now and had always been so forthright in the past. He *believed* she was Xandra Fortune, the French fashion model and orphan the world saw. And he *didn't* believe she was pregnant.

The irony almost choked her. "I am not lying."

His cynical smile galvanized her into action. She dug in her purse and grabbed the white stick that proved her pregnancy. She waved it in front of him. "One blue line means yes to a pregnancy."

She did not know exactly what reaction she had expected, but it was not the volatile, fury filled one she got.

He grabbed her wrist, lifting the hand with the pregnancy test, his body vibrating with palpable anger. "You dare to show this to me?"

What was wrong with him? "Yes, I dare. I won't let you ignore the reality of your baby just because you've decided it's time to marry another woman."

A nerve ticked in his jaw. "Do you think I am stupid? You cannot possibly be pregnant with *my* child."

"The condom broke, remember?" He should. He'd made enough of it at the time.

"That was before your period and we did not have sex again until two days ago." The grip on her wrist tightened painfully. "Tell me you are not pregnant. Tell me this—" he shook her hand "—is some kind of joke."

"You're hurting me," she whispered as tears clogged her throat and burned her eyes.

A flash went off and he let her go, throwing her arm from him with disgust. She watched out of the periphery of her vision as one of Dimitri's security men took off after the photographer. "It's not a lie. I am pregnant."

If anything, he seemed to swell with more anger. "It is not my child."

For a moment his words paralyzed her. How could he doubt it was his child? She'd never had another lover. He knew it. "It is."

His face contorted with revulsion. "All this time you have been haranguing me for planning to marry Phoebe, you have known you took another man to your bed. Who is it?''

His shouted question made her jump in fright. Dimitri never lost his cool. He hated scenes and putting on a public display was anathema to him.

"There is no other man."

"The evidence is not in your favor." His voice had dropped to freezing levels.

"I don't know how it can be, but it is."

"I had planned to be generous, give you the apartment. I thought you deserved it, but I'll be damned if I'm going to pay for your lover's lifestyle and support his bastard child. I am not that stupid." He grabbed the papers off the table, but tossed the box at her. "This should be a sufficiently memorable token for services rendered."

She shoved the box aside. "There is no other man!"

His face closed up and terror coursed through her. He did not believe her. "You can have the tests done."

He stood up. "Be assured I will demand them if you attempt to sue for any kind of support."

Alexandra gulped, trying to get enough air. Trying not to vomit, but the pain was so intense that she wasn't sure she could win the battle. Her arms were wrapped tightly around her middle and she still felt like she was going to fly apart into a thousand broken little pieces.

To have the gift of their child so brutally rejected hurt almost beyond bearing.

She whimpered.

Whipping her hand to her mouth, she blocked the sound with her fist. She did not want to let him see her weakness.

"You have twenty-four hours to vacate the apartment." He gave her one last sulfuric glare, spun on his heel and left.

Alexandra paced from one side of the living room to the other. She'd called Dimitri's cell phone at least a dozen times and gotten his message service every time. She'd left messages with the operator, at his Paris office, at his office in Athens, even with his grandfather's housekeeper.

Every message had said the same thing. *Please call.*

He hadn't. Not all day yesterday as she vacillated between tortured tears and blazing fury. Not through a sleepless night when she had tossed and turned in a bed too big for comfort without him in it. She'd tried to rest for the baby's sake, but every time she closed her eyes images of him telling her he planned to marry intruded, or worse…his expression of revulsion when she'd told him she was pregnant.

It was now close to one o'clock in the afternoon and she'd spent the last hour calling every contact number she had for him again. It hadn't done any good. She couldn't sit down. She was so strung out and edgy, she felt like she'd taken a couple of the diet pills some of her fellow models used to control their appetite.

One thought played itself over and over again in her brain. Dimitri believed she'd taken another lover. What kind of trust was that? He really did think she was some kind of slut.

The thought sent her to her knees only to hop up again at the sound of a key turning in the lock. She flew to the door. He'd come back. Relief surged through her in unstoppable waves. He'd realized how idiotic he'd been to believe she could make love to another man.

She wrenched the door open. "Dim—" Her voice

choked off mid word. It wasn't Dimitri at the door. "Who the hell are you?" she demanded in English before remembering where she was and repeating her question in French.

The stocky bald man pushed his way into the apartment, followed by an efficient looking woman and another man, this one lanky and sandy haired. The woman spoke. "I am Mr. Petronides's facilities manager. I am here to oversee your vacation of the apartment."

Alexandra barely made it to the bathroom before she lost the little bit of food she'd forced herself to eat that day.

When she came out, the brunette was directing the two men in the packing of Alexandra's things with an officious looking clipboard in one hand and a pen in the other. The facilities manager used her pen to point at a small Lladro figurine Dimitri had bought Alexandra when they were in Barcelona together.

The bald man picked up the statuette and began wrapping it in paper before putting it in one of the numerous boxes the moving team must have brought with them. Alexandra stood in appalled fascination as every item she could claim as her own was packed in a similarly efficient manner from the living room.

The last three days had been nightmarish, but this was beyond a nightmare. It was so horrifyingly real, she almost buckled from the pain of it.

"He sent you to evict me?" She asked the words in a bare whisper, but the other woman heard.

She turned to Alexandra, her face impassive. "I have been sent to facilitate your move, yes."

"Have you evicted many of his ex-lovers?" Alexandra asked.

The other woman's eyes twitched. "Your relationship

with Mr. Petronides is not my business. I am simply following through on my instructions.''

''War criminals say the same thing in their defense.''

Her mouth tightening, the brunette turned away without answering. Alexandra did not push it. Instead, she marched into the bedroom she had shared with Dimitri and started packing her clothes. She didn't want those men touching them. She already felt violated by their presence and the way they went through *her* home removing *her* things, removing traces of *her*.

Two hours later, the packing was done. Alexandra returned to the living room and surveyed the neatly piled boxes the two men were preparing to transport out of the apartment. Were they going to take them down to the lobby and leave them there? Out onto the street?

Suddenly emotions that had gone numb in the face of Dimitri's cruel ejection of her from his life, came back to life and Alexandra shouted, ''Stop!'' as the bald man went to pick up one of the boxes.

The man stopped.

''Some of the items you packed don't belong to me. You'll have to wait while I sort through the boxes and take them out.''

''I had a very specific list from Mr. Petronides,'' the brunette began to say.

''I don't care.'' Alexandra stood to her full five feet, nine inches and glared the other woman down. ''I'm not taking his property with me.''

The movers must have read her determination on her face because they didn't attempt to dissuade her again. It took forty-five minutes, but in the end she had removed every single thing Dimitri had ever given her. She'd gone through her clothes as well, chucking sexy lingerie from her suitcases along with designer dresses...anything and everything he had bought.

When she was done, there was a pile of objects mixed with crumpled manila newsprint on the living room floor along with two stacks of neatly folded clothes.

"There's one more thing."

The brunette just nodded, her eyes registering some emotion after watching Alexandra's feverish attempt to purge her things of all items related to her ex-lover.

Alexandra picked up her purse and pulled out the white stick she'd replaced yesterday after the disastrous confrontation with Dimitri along with the jewelry case he'd left lying on the café table. She dropped them both on top of the lingerie pile. She stood up and grabbed the handle of her suitcase, slung the matching overnight case over her shoulder and exited the apartment.

Alexandra waited a week to hear from Dimitri, hoping time would calm him to the point of rationality. Seven days after she'd been evicted from their apartment, she read an article in the society column announcing his up-coming wedding to Phoebe Leonides. The girl looked about nineteen and as innocent as any virginal bride should be.

Alexandra checked out of the hotel she'd been staying in, arranged for her possessions to be shipped to the U.S., terminated her contract with her modeling agency, closed her Xandra Fortune checking account, canceled her credit cards under that name and bought a ticket back to the states in the name of Alexandra Dupree.

Xandra Fortune, fashion model and ex-lover of Greek billionaire, Dimitri Petronides, ceased to exist.

A little over two months later, Alexandra walked out of the prenatal clinic into the hot, sticky air of early autumn

in New York City. She glanced down at the snapshot of
her recent ultrasound. She'd put the videotape in her bag,
but hadn't been able to tuck the photo away. She was
enthralled with this proof of the baby growing in her
womb. The baby she could not yet feel or even see in
her only slightly thickened waistline.

It was a boy. A part of Dimitri Petronides she was
free to love, someone who would return her love. Even
weakened by constant morning sickness and exhausted
from her pregnancy, she wanted to shout for joy.

Desperately wanting to share her news with someone,
she flipped open her cell phone and dialed her sister's
number. She got the answering machine and opted not
to leave a message. She could tell Madeleine the news
when she went home later. She considered and discarded
the idea of calling her mother. Alexandra was not up to
another dose of "You've brought shame to the family
name."

Compulsion she could not deny had her dialing the
number to the Paris apartment. There had been no news
of Dimitri's wedding in the New York society pages.
Fool that she was, she couldn't stop herself from looking
and even more foolishly hoping. Had he come to his
senses? Called off the wedding?

Perhaps the latter was too much to hope for, but surely
after two months he would have had enough time to
calm down and realize Alexandra would never have
been unfaithful to him.

The phone rang several times and Alexandra remembered belatedly it would be the dinner hour over there.
Perhaps he was out, or not in Paris at all. She let the
phone continue to ring, knowing she didn't have the
courage to call his cell. For some reason this was news

she needed to tell him when he was in the apartment they had shared.

The other line picked up. "Hello?"

Alexandra almost dropped her phone. It was a woman's voice at the other end of the line. She forced her vocal chords to work, praying the unfamiliar voice was that of a new housekeeper and not Dimitri's newest woman. "Hello. Is Mr. Petronides available, please?"

"I'm sorry, he's out. This is Mrs. Petronides. Can I help you or would you like to leave a message?"

Mrs. Petronides. Alexandra stopped breathing. The bastard had gone through with it. He'd married another woman while Alexandra was pregnant with his child. Funny, until that very moment, she hadn't truly believed he would do it. And it was only in the absence of all hope that she realized how much she'd been living on the unspoken faith in a man who cared nothing for her and clearly never had.

"Are you there?"

"Yes."

"Did you want to leave a message for my husband?"

"No. I…" The words simply trailed into nothingness as the joy that had buoyed her up since discovering she carried Dimitri's son drained away.

"Who's calling please?" The young woman, Phoebe Leonides, no…Phoebe Petronides now, sounded impatient.

Because Alexandra was so emotionally devastated, she answered the other woman's question without thought. She couldn't think. Her brain had ceased to function. She gave the name an occupant of the Paris apartment would expect to hear. "Xandra Fortune."

"Miss Fortune, where are you? Dimitrius has been looking for you. He's desperate about the baby."

Dimitri had told his wife about her, about their baby? Alexandra pulled the phone from her ear and stared at it in her hand as if she didn't know how it had gotten there. She could hear the woman's voice, but not the words she was saying. She sounded frantic.

Alexandra cut the connection without putting the phone back to her ear.

CHAPTER THREE

DIMITRI took a sip of his neat whiskey and walked out onto the terrace of the New York high-rise apartment. It was empty, no doubt due to the chill in the air brought on by November's cooling temperatures.

He'd come late to the holiday party, at the insistence of a business acquaintance who'd told him the host was an investment banker he thought Dimitri should meet. For the past four months, Dimitri had had very little interest in making money. He'd had little interest in anything, but finding the mother of his child.

He was in New York because that was her last known whereabouts. She'd had her things shipped to a Manhattan receiving office and picked them up on the day of their arrival. One day before he had instigated a search for her. After that, there had been nothing. His investigators had been unable to find a single lead.

She'd canceled her contract with her modeling agency. She'd even closed her credit cards and checking account. No one had seen or heard from Xandra Fortune in three months.

Well, that was not strictly true. She'd called the Paris apartment four weeks ago and spoken to Phoebe. Xandra had hung up without saying why she'd called or answering Phoebe's questions about where she was. The call had been placed on an untraceable cell phone.

Dimitri still cursed whenever he thought of that ill-fated phone call. Would she have told him where she was if he had been there to answer the phone?

The sound of voices drifted out onto the almost deserted terrace and he asked himself why he'd bothered to come. He spun on his heel, intending to go when a woman caught his eye. She had her back to him. Long curling blond hair reached to the center of her back, a back that looked much too familiar. Then she moved, gripping the balcony railing and letting her head fall back as she took a deep breath of air.

"Xandra!"

She spun around to face him and his heart tightened in a painful knot, for although the woman had enough surface resemblance to Xandra to be her sister, she wasn't the model.

She smiled, even white teeth gleaming in the cool glow of the outdoor lighting. "Hello. I didn't realize anyone was out here."

"I came for the solitude," he admitted.

Her smile flashed again. "I know what you mean. I adore socializing, but once in a while the crush gets to me and I just need to breathe some air that's all my own."

He felt himself smiling for the first time in months. "Then I'll leave you to it."

She waved her hand. "There's no need. I don't mind sharing my little oasis of quiet. You said you knew Xandra?"

"Yes. I know her."

"She was an amazing model, wasn't she? She had just the right combination of innocence and passion to shoot her to supermodel status. It's too bad she refused to take any New York commissions."

"She prefers working in Europe."

Something odd passed across the woman's face. "Yes, I suppose she did."

"You keep talking about her in the past tense." Had Xandra given up modeling for motherhood?

"That's because Xandra Fortune is gone."

Everything inside him went still. "What do you mean gone?"

The blonde sighed. "According to my sister, Xandra Fortune is dead, if not buried six feet under."

The words had the effect of multiple body blows and he felt his knees begin to buckle. He reached out blindly for the balcony railing and it was only by sheer force of will that he remained standing. *"She's dead?"*

He tried to breathe, but his lungs refused to cooperate. He felt the whiskey glass in his hand break and the sharp pain of one jagged edge pressing into his hand.

"Oh, my word. Are you all right?" The woman's voice was filled with concern. "Wait right there. I'll get something for the cut and to clean up the glass."

He looked down at the blood beading against the dark skin of his hand and could not connect it to anything he felt because all he felt was numbness. Xandra was dead and his baby with her. That thought pounded through his consciousness with the power of an express train pushing away all other considerations.

It could have been minutes or hours later, but the woman returned armed with a first-aid kit and the maid behind her carrying a bowl of water and some small towels.

"Put those down on the table and close the door on your way out," the woman instructed the maid. She gave Dimitri a small smile. "I don't want an incident at the party. Hunter, my husband, doesn't like scenes."

"You said Xandra was dead." Perhaps he had misheard her.

"Yes." She bathed his hand and fixed a plaster over

the small cut with gentle efficiency. "I didn't mean to upset you. I forget that others don't know…" Her voice trailed off and he didn't press her to continue.

He didn't care if anyone else knew Xandra had died. "Was it…" He swallowed. "The baby?"

Her hands stilled in their task of putting the first-aid implements to rights. "How did you know about the baby?" Her light brown gaze pinned him and her charming air had transformed to one of suspicion.

"She told me."

"You're Dimitri Petronides?" The woman spit his name out of her mouth as if it were a foul tasting substance.

"Yes."

He didn't see the blow coming, but he felt it. Her hand landed against the side of his face with enough force to turn his head and make him stagger back a step.

"You filthy pig! I'd like to strangle you with my bare hands. How you have the gall to come here, to my home after the way you treated my sister."

"What the hell is going on out here?" Another man came storming out onto the terrace. A veritable blond giant. "What have you said to upset my wife?"

"Hunter!" The woman threw herself at her husband. "It's Dimitri Petronides. He's the one. You've got to get him out of here. If Allie sees him, she'll have a relapse. She's just started sleeping at night. Do something!"

None of the woman's words or actions had made sense since she'd told Dimitri Xandra was dead, but then how could anything make sense in the face of that devastating fact?

He turned to go, more than willing to abandon the scene.

*   *   *

Alexandra could hear her sister's voice raised in agitation from where she sat chatting with one of Hunter's many business associates in the penthouse's living room. She excused herself and stood up. Madeleine's voice had lowered to the point where Alexandra could not make out what her sister was saying, but the urgency was still there.

She walked through the dining room tastefully decorated in autumn colors for the Thanksgiving holiday and out onto the balcony. Madeleine was gripping Hunter's biceps and saying something about getting rid of someone. A bowl of water, tinged pink and a bloodied towel lay on the table to her right and the smell of spilled whiskey permeated the air. A small pile of broken glass lay winking in the outside lights near the outer wall of the terrace.

"Madeleine, are you all right, *chérie?*"

Madeleine whipped around, her expression horror stricken. She rushed to Alexandra and grabbed her wrist. "Come on, Allie." She started tugging.

Alexandra resisted simply because she didn't understand the urgency in her sister's voice and wanted to know the reason for it. She looked down the length of the balcony to see if she could discover the source of her sister's agitation and froze. Dimitri Petronides was heading in the opposite direction, toward the sliding glass doors leading into Hunter's study.

He stopped at the open doorway and turned. "I didn't mean to upset your wife," he said to Hunter in a voice unlike anything she had ever heard out of Dimitri's mouth.

His gaze flicked over the tableau she made with her sister pulling frantically against her arm.

His eyes appeared unfocused, as if he wasn't even seeing them. ''I'll see myself out.''

Then he was gone.

Again.

He'd walked away from her for the second time without a backward glance. It was no consolation that this time he would have been hard pressed to recognize her.

''I'm sorry, Allie. I don't know how he came to be here. Are you going to be all right?'' Madeleine's voice buzzed in Alexandra's ears. ''I slapped him.'' Her sister's words finally registered.

''You what?''

''I slapped him and I called him a pig.''

Alexandra almost smiled. ''He deserved it.''

''Yes, he did.''

''How did you know who he was?''

''I told him you were dead, I mean Xandra Fortune. Anyway, he asked if it was because of the baby and I just knew.''

''You told him Xandra was dead?''

''Yes, she did, but it's not true is it? You're alive and I'd like to shake you both until your teeth rattle.'' Dimitri's fury filled voice sent Alexandra's nerves into overdrive.

Madeleine dropped Alexandra's wrist in shock. ''Go away!'' she shouted at Dimitri.

He towered over them, his skin an unnatural shade of gray, his eyes registering anger and a brief moment of vulnerability that disappeared before Alexandra could be certain of its existence. ''I'm not going anywhere. In fact, I think it is you and your husband who need to go so Xandra and I may speak in private of affairs that do not concern you.''

Madeleine opened her mouth to speak, but Alexandra

forestalled her. She pivoted her body so she faced Dimitri fully and fixed him with a bored stare. "My name is Alexandra Dupree and I'm sure you and I have nothing to discuss."

Since leaving her Xandra Fortune persona behind, she'd run into former colleagues and none of them had recognized her. She'd had her hair cut short and dyed back to the rather mousy-brown color she'd been born with. She'd ditched the green contact lenses and her body at five months pregnant in no way resembled the willow thinness of Xandra Fortune's trademark figure.

There was no reason she couldn't bluff this confrontation with Dimitri out. And a very good reason why she wanted to. She'd thought and thought about why he would tell his wife about her and the baby and the only logical solution she'd been able to come up with was that Dimitri had decided that though he no longer wanted his ex-lover, he did want their child.

Something dangerous flashed in Dimitri's indigo blue eyes. "Do not play games with me."

"I am not playing any games. If you do not believe me about who I am, I can show you identification. I've been Alexandra Dupree my whole life. I should know." She deliberately infused her voice with a New Orleans accent, one she hadn't spoken with since being sent to convent boarding school in France at the age of eight.

"Ten minutes ago I believed you to be dead."

"I can confirm without question that Xandra Fortune is indeed dead, but I am not and I am Alexandra Dupree."

He didn't even look disconcerted. "You may be Alexandra Dupree, but you are also Xandra Fortune and how you believe you could deny such truth to me, the man who knows you more intimately than any other, I cannot understand.'' His usual flawless English was heavily accented with Greek intonation.

"I assure you, you do not know me intimately at all.'' And that was the truth. If he had truly known her, he could never have suspected the baby had been fathered by someone else.

Terrible rage reflected in Dimitri's eyes before he leaned forward and swept her high against his chest, his arms as tight and inflexible as steel bands.

Madeleine shrieked, "Put her down!"

Hunter strode forward to grab Dimitri's shoulder.

Dimitri glared at him, his body tense with primitive masculine aggression. "Take your hand off me.''

"I won't allow you to take my sister-in-law out of this apartment against her will.''

The entire situation was unreal. Dimitrius Petronides doing something so uncool as to attempt to kidnap a pregnant woman from a party was beyond the scope of her imagination, much less believable reality.

Dimitri looked down at her, his blue gaze compelling agreement. "Tell him you want to come with me.''

She glared back at him. "I don't.''

Dimitri stiffened and Hunter became more menacing, but in his fury, Dimitri shrugged off Hunter's restraining hold as if it were nothing more than a wispy cobweb. He spun to face Hunter. "I'm not going to hurt her. She's mine. She's pregnant with my child and we're going to talk.''

After that, neither Dimitri nor Hunter spoke for what seemed like several minutes, but was in all probability only seconds. Then something passed between the two men and much to Madeleine's dismay and Alexandra's irritation Hunter nodded.

"You can talk to her, but you'll have to do it here.''

Alexandra tried to shove herself out of Dimitri's arms. "I'm not talking to him."

His hold tightened. "Be careful. If you fall, you could hurt the baby."

"What do you care about my baby?"

If possible, his expression turned grimmer. "I care."

Those two words scared her more than the thought of giving birth to a child. He was going to try to take her baby from her. She knew it. "I'm not giving you and your little Greek paragon wife my baby. I'm not!"

He shook his head. "Talk. Xandra. We need to talk."

"You didn't even believe the baby was yours at first," she said, giving up any hope at deceiving him about her identity.

Emotion passed across his chiseled features. "I do now."

"What changed your mind?" she demanded, ceasing her struggle against the increasing pressure of his hold.

He smelled like whiskey, expensive aftershave and sweat. Something had made Dimitri sweat. In fact, his hairline still showed evidence of moisture. The thought of losing his baby must have really destroyed him. She could almost feel sorry for him, but she refused to be so weak. He'd denied his paternity of their baby. He deserved what he got.

"I spoke to a doctor. He told me it was actually quite common for a woman to have one or even two menses after conceiving a child."

"So you believed some stranger over me. I'm impressed, Dimitri. It certainly shows where our relationship fit in the scheme of your life."

"He's not a stranger. He's a friend."

Who cared how well he knew the stupid doctor? "I'm not giving you my baby!" she reiterated while inside she cursed the doctor who had put her bond with her child at risk like this.

"If you don't put my sister down this instant and leave my home, I'm calling the police," Madeleine interrupted.

Eyes deadly with intent, Dimitri met Madeleine's gaze with his own inflexible one. "Go ahead." He turned to Hunter. "I'm not going anywhere without her."

Hunter sighed. "You can talk out here. We'll close off the doors to the house so you'll have some privacy."

Alexandra shuddered. She didn't want privacy with Dimitri. "If I have to talk to you, I'd rather do it somewhere public."

"You don't have to talk to him at all," Madeleine's angry voice interjected.

Hunter squeezed Madeleine's shoulder. "She's pregnant with his child, my love. They have to talk."

Her sister turned on her husband with murder in her eye. "I suppose that's some macho code all arrogant men try to live by, but I'm not standing by and watching him rip my sister into emotional shreds again. Don't you remember how she was when she got here?"

As much as she loved her sister and appreciated Madeleine's loyalty, Alexandra did not want Dimitri to know how much he had hurt her. Her pride would not take it. "Put me down. We can go to Casamir," she said, naming a French restaurant on B Avenue.

Dimitri and Madeleine said *no* at the same time. Alexandra opted to deal with her sister first. "Maddy, I want this settled."

Madeleine's eyes filled with tears. "I don't want you hurt again."

Alexandra shook her head, very certain of that if nothing else. "He can't hurt me anymore. I despise him."

Dimitri's body jerked.

She ignored the reaction and asked him, "Why can't we go to Casamir?"

"We tried to talk nicely in a public venue once and it did not work. Did you see the photos? They were all over the papers the week after my engagement to Phoebe was announced. *Wealthy Greek Tycoon Argues with Secret Pregnant Paramour.* My grandfather relapsed and had to have emergency by-pass surgery."

Alexandra stifled her urge to offer sympathy. Dimitri got nothing from her from this point forward. Nothing.

"Talk out here, Allie. You don't want your circumstances bandied about any more than Dimitri does. If pictures of you make it into the scandal rags here, your mother may not have a heart attack, but the hissy fit she'll throw won't be much of an improvement and it will all come down on your head."

Madeleine glared at her husband, but agreed. "Hunter's right. If you are going to talk to this swine it might as well be here where no sleazy journalists are waiting to quote an overheard conversation or take damaging pictures."

Dimitri's patience was wearing thin and Alexandra could feel his anger mounting. Some things, it seemed, had not changed. She could still read him like the other half of herself. She found the thought so disturbing, she buried it immediately.

"You're right. Mother is already prepared to disown me and make up some story about my early demise. We'll talk here."

She would have mistaken the breath Dimitri expelled as a sigh of relief, but she no longer believed he was capable of feeling enough vulnerability to be relieved.

With a few dire warnings to Dimitri and concerned

looks at Alexandra, Madeleine allowed Hunter to lead
her from the terrace after turning on the small gas outdoor fireplace. The sound of metal sliding against metal
indicated one set of doors closing. A minute of silent
waiting and the second set of doors closed from the inside of the apartment. As the vertical blinds slid across
the doorway and then turned to create a visual barrier
against the rest of the party, Alexandra felt trapped.

She was alone with a man she used to love—a man
she no longer trusted.

Dimitri didn't speak. He didn't move. He just stared
at her and then at the football-size bump that indicated
their baby living and growing beneath her heart. Tension
arced between them and she became aware of the feel
of his hard, muscular chest against her side.

"Put me down."

He seemed to snap out of a trance and his gaze shifted
to hers. "Your eyes are golden. They used to be green."

"Color contacts."

"Even at night?"

"The lights were dim, or off."

"You cut your hair."

"Yes."

"It's darker."

She shrugged. He, of all people should know her natural hair color. He'd been the only one to see it in the
last six years since she'd had her first bleach job and
landed her first modeling contract.

"I like it."

That made her angry. He had no right to like anything
about her anymore. He was a married man. "I don't
care."

His eyes narrowed and his mouth set in a firm line.

She refused to cower before the signs of his anger.

"As fascinating as this discussion is, I thought you had more important issues you wanted to talk about."

He nodded. He gently lowered her into a wicker armchair before seating himself in its twin on the other side of a small wicker and glass table. Both were well away from the broken whiskey glass and first-aid supplies, but near the fireplace whose gas lit flames generated some heat.

Contrarily, she missed the warmth of his body as a slight autumn breeze caught the strands of her chin-length hair and lifted them to chilling effect. She shivered.

"You are cold. We should talk inside."

Where someone might hear? "No. It was just a breeze."

He shucked out of his coat and tucked it around her shoulders before she knew what was happening. She tried to shrug it off, but he held it in place by the lapels. "Do not be stubborn."

His nearness was doing something to her hard won emotional distance so she agreed in order to get him to back off. It didn't do a lot of good. The coat carried his scent and warmed from his body, it was like having his arms closed protectively around her. Stifling the image that thought provoked, she focused on getting down to business.

She smoothed her oversized, sage green cable knit sweater over the baby, reminding herself that possession was nine-tenths of the law and no one could deny that right now, she was the one in possession of their baby. "What is it exactly you think we have to talk about?" she asked, going on the offensive.

He looked her in the eye, his blue gaze dark with purpose. "I want my child."

CHAPTER FOUR

HE wanted her baby.

She had suspected it since her call to the Paris apartment, but hearing him say it was like being tossed into a black hole and having all the air sucked out of the universe at one time.

She put her hands protectively over her tummy as if by doing so she could somehow prevent him from carrying through on his monstrous plan. "You can't have him."

"You say *him*. Do you mean to say you know he is a boy?"

Should she lie? Would he fight any less ruthlessly for a daughter? The implacable expression on his face said not.

"Yes."

"How do you know?"

"I had an ultrasound at four months."

An expression of dawning understanding came over his hardened features. "That's why you called the apartment."

She refused to answer.

His hands fisted against the Italian suit wool covering his thighs. "You were going to tell me our baby was to be a boy." He sounded astonished by the fact.

Why shouldn't he be? He'd treated her like the lowest of the low, denied his paternity, ditched her to marry another woman and evicted her from their apartment like a bad tenant ninety days past lease. And she'd called to tell him the sex of their child. How stupidly sentimental could any one woman be?

An expression like grief passed over his face, though what he had to grieve about, she could not imagine. "And you spoke to Phoebe."

Why bother answering? He knew the details already.

"You refused to tell her where you were."

"Do you blame me?"

His jaw clenched. "Funnily enough. Yes. I can blame you. Phoebe begged you to tell her where you were and you refused. I've spent months of fruitless searching and hired no less than five world-class detective agencies, only to be told by all of them that Xandra Fortune ceased to exist."

"They were right."

"Yet, here you are."

"No. Here you see Alexandra Dupree. I will never be Xandra Fortune again." She would never allow herself to be vulnerable to the man she had loved as Xandra again, either.

"You told me you were an orphan."

She felt her mouth twist cynically. "No. That is what your agency told you when you had me investigated as a suitable candidate to be your lover. I just never denied it."

"You created an entire persona for yourself."

"Yes."

"You lied to me every day of our association."

Association? Was that anything like a relationship gone sour? "I did not lie to you."

"You let me call you Xandra."

"Many models use a working name."

"Only you lived a life completely separate from this

reality I now find in a New York apartment. That woman, Madeleine, she is your sister?''

"Yes. Hunter is her husband.''

His brows rose in mockery. "I had figured that out.''

She clenched her fists so she wouldn't hit him.

He laughed, but it was a sound without mirth. "Don't try it. Your sister already slapped me.'' He lifted his plastered hand as a silent indicator of that wound. "I'm in no mood to sustain further injury.''

"Poor you,'' she jeered.

"Keep pushing it and my temper will override my patience.''

Remembering the inimical fury he'd exhibited the day she told him of her pregnancy, she shivered. "I used to think you were such a cool guy, no scenes, no temper tantrums, all sleek sophisticated Greek male.''

"Do not forget rich.''

"I don't care about your filthy money. I never did.''

"Yet it will be difficult for you to win against it, should you attempt to withhold my child from me.''

Fear tried to take hold, but she refused to give into it. "You don't scare me. This isn't Greece. You can't take my baby away from me just because you're rich and male. United States family law is heavily balanced in the mother's favor.'' She'd looked into it as soon as she'd hit New York. She'd known even then that if Dimitri ever decided to claim her child, she would be facing difficulties ahead.

"Perhaps, but can you afford the constant legal battles? The draining expense of hiring top-notch lawyers to plead your case.''

The picture he painted was a bleak one. "I'll do whatever it takes to keep my child.''

"Anything?''

"Yes! Anything."

"Then come with your baby to my home."

That sent her to her feet in a hurry. "You arrogant toad! Do you honestly believe I would go anywhere with you after everything that has happened?"

Her stomach churned. Did he think she was such a dope that she would let him set her and their son up somewhere convenient while he lived happy families with Phoebe? Another ugly thought followed the last one. "I won't be your mistress," she hissed with enough venom to slay him.

He too shot out of his chair. "I'm not looking for a mistress."

"Good, because I won't be one. Not ever. I learned all I wanted to know about having uncommitted sex with a guy so primitive he should be in a museum. The next time I have sex with a man, I'm going to have a ring on my finger and an avowal of love to go with it!"

"Just who is this man?" he demanded in a near roar.

"I don't know, but when I find him, he won't be anything like you!"

"You think not?" Then he reached out and grabbed the lapels of his suit jacket again, yanking her to him. "I think this mythical man will be just like me because he will be me. No other man touches the mother of my child."

He'd said the words a breath above her lips and then closed the distance. And the electric current of desire was there, waiting, lurking in her deepest subconscious to come to the fore with the first touch of his mouth to hers.

She went under so fast, she didn't even have time to despise herself for her weakness. His mouth moved over

hers with truly possessive passion and she responded like
a woman deprived of physical intimacy for years.

Her hands locked around his neck, her body stretched
to press itself to his and her mouth opened in serious
invitation. He took it and deepened the kiss even as his
hands caressed her back, pressing her closer to him, letting her feel his heat and his excitement. Blatant evidence of that excitement brought her to her senses and
she shoved herself away from him so fast and so hard,
she stumbled backward and fell flat on her bottom.

He was on his knees beside in her in a second. "You
foolish woman! You could have hurt yourself. Are you
trying to kill our son? Are you all right?" His hands
were doing a hasty examination of her and her body was
getting the wrong message entirely from those imper-
sonal touches.

She slapped his hands away. "Stop it. I'm fine." Her
bottom was sore, but she wasn't about to tell him that.
"Babies are resilient. I'm not going to lose him from
such a small fall." *Oh Lord, please let that be true.*

"You would take such a risk?" He glared at her.
"What other risks have you taken with our child?"

If she'd had a gun, she would have shot him, or at
least at him…to scare him a little and wipe that conde-
scending look of censure off his face. "It's not my fault
you acted like a lecher and kissed me. What was I supposed to do, tolerate it?"

He swelled with affronted pride. "You have never
merely tolerated my kiss in your life."

She had no argument to that, so she didn't try making
one. "Married men are not supposed to kiss women
other than their wives," she said instead.

He shrugged. "I agree. Does this worry you?"

Was he for real? Of course it worried her. He was

married to Phoebe and he'd just soul-kissed Alexandra. "Am I crazy, or are you?" she asked, feeling helplessly bewildered.

His mouth twisted in a grimace. "I have been crazy since the first report from the private investigators trying to locate you. They had not a single lead and you had disappeared in one of the largest cities in the world."

He tucked the suit coat around her slender shoulders once again, then leaned down and lifted her in his arms. Was there something about imminent fatherhood that made the male of the species go all basic? She could remember only one other time he'd carried her during their year together and that had been one night she'd had a little too much champagne and fallen asleep in the car on the way home.

Yet, tonight, he'd picked her up like he owned her. Twice. "Please put me down, Dimitri." It was a sign of how vulnerable she felt that she made it a request instead of a demand.

Either way, he did not comply. "I do not think I should. You are too volatile right now."

She closed her eyes in frustration. "I'll control myself if you keep your hands and lips to yourself."

"I cannot promise this."

"Poor Phoebe. Does she know what an unfaithful letch she is married to?"

"Phoebe is married to a man of absolute honor," he replied, his voice laced with furious affront.

"You? Don't make me laugh," she scorned. A man with integrity did not marry one woman after impregnating another.

Dimitri sat down, keeping Alexandra pinned in his lap. His blue gaze scorched into hers. "You believe I am married to Phoebe? And you believe I have no honor?'' The last was said with escalating anger.

''I suppose you're going to try to tell me you're not married to your little Greek paragon.''

''This is true. I am not.''

Alexandra closed her eyes. She didn't know why, but she hadn't expected him to lie to her. She opened them again and stared into his deceitful face. ''She told me she was your wife, so you can just forget about the smoothy deceptions.''

''She would not have told you she was my wife.'' His voice was filled with such conviction that Alexandra thought back to the devastating phone call.

''She told me she was Mrs. Petronides.''

''But then she told you she was married to my brother.''

''What?''

''She told you she had wed my brother.''

''She did no such thing!'' But she could have. Alexandra remembered the voice still talking as she'd ended the call.

Dimitri wouldn't let her look away from him, his compelling eyes holding hers hostage. ''She did.''

''But…''

''She also pleaded with you to tell her where you were.''

Alexandra remembered that part. ''I wasn't about to have a heart-to-heart with your new wife.''

''She is not my wife.''

''Prove it.''

In his shock at her demand, Dimitri's grip loosened and Alexandra extricated herself from his lap, this time much more carefully. ''You say you are not married to Phoebe Petronides. Well, I don't trust you anymore,

Dimitri. If you want me to believe it, you'll have to bring me proof.''

He shot to his feet again, all outraged male. "How dare you question my word?''

"You wouldn't believe how easy it is,'' she admitted.

That seemed to shake him. "I will get you the proof you require,'' he said angrily.

"Fine. Until then, I suggest you go.''

"I am not letting you out of my sight again.''

"What do you propose, setting up camp outside my sister's door and dogging my every footstep?''

"Count on it, but I have no desire to sleep in a hallway. You can come with me to my suite.''

"No way. I'm not staying in a hotel room with you.''

"There are two bedrooms, though there was a time you would not have required the other one.''

She glared at his, to her mind, savagely insensitive reminder. "Forget it. I'm not going.''

"Then I will stay here. It is a large apartment. I'm sure your sister has a spare room I could use.''

She felt flummoxed. "You can't stay here. Madeleine would have a hissy fit. She hates you.''

He shrugged his broad shoulders. "Speaking of hissy fits, your brother-in-law implied your mother would have one if you were featured in a scandalous article.''

Alexandra couldn't prevent her eyes from rolling in exasperation. "Yes.'' She'd spent six years living as someone else to protect her mother's sense of family dignity. *Dupree women did not work.*

Only this generation of Dupree women would have been out on the street if one of them hadn't ignored the old money heritage and gotten a job to support the family. The cousin of a friend from school had offered her a modeling contract. She'd taken it with one proviso...she work anonymously under an assumed name. He'd gone one better and helped her create Xandra Fortune, French orphan turned fashion model.

Dimitri was speaking again. "She would be most upset to see an exposé interview with her daughter's discarded tycoon lover and rejected father of her child."

Her body didn't know whether to go faint or boil with fury at his implied threat and twisting of the facts. "I didn't discard you. You dumped me to marry Phoebe, the Greek *virgin* bride, or don't you remember?"

"I am not married to Phoebe."

"You don't have to have committed a murder to be guilty of a crime."

Instead of getting angrier, he smiled. "Are you saying you believe I did not marry her?"

"No!"

"You still require proof?"

"Yes."

"Then you'll have to convince your sister to give me a bed for the night because I'm not letting you out of my sight."

"And if I don't, you're going to make sure my family's name gets a good smearing in the tabloids, is that it?" she asked with all the derision at her disposal.

He didn't even flinch. "Yes."

"I despise you."

"Not hate?"

"No. I don't love you anymore, but I refuse to hate you. Part of you is in my child and I won't ever have my child believing there is anything about him I could hate." Her son deserved better than a mother eaten up by bitterness.

A look she could not decipher settled on Dimitri's

chiseled features. "That is commendable. Now, shall we talk to your sister about my accommodation?"

In the end, Alexandra decided it would be better to accompany Dimitri to his suite. The mere thought of trying to work out the current complications in her life with her younger sister breathing fire at Dimitri left her cold. Alexandra did not want Madeleine and Hunter forced into a position of enmity with a man of Dimitri's wealth and power because of her.

Going to Dimitri's suite was the only workable solution. It wasn't going to be all that bad, she decided. She didn't need to worry about Dimitri getting to her. She was well and truly over him. The kiss had just been physical reaction to memories and she wouldn't let it happen again.

All that was left between them was to determine how they would handle his role in her son's life.

If anyone had asked Alexandra two days ago the chances of her sitting down to breakfast with Dimitri in his hotel suite, she would have said nil. Nada. Zilch. Absolutely not one. Yet, here they sat. She pushed her eggs and fruit around the plate of breakfast room service had provided minutes earlier. He eyed her with calculating regard.

She knew what he saw. A positive hag. She hadn't been able to sleep again last night, not with the knowledge that Dimitri rested on the other side of the wall. Her eyes looked bruised while her complexion wore its usual sallow tint from her pregnancy. Most women finished with morning sickness at three to four months. Not Alexandra. She still woke up every day feeling like she had the flu and she was in her fifth month.

Her one consolation was Dimitri didn't look much

better. She'd been too overwrought to notice it the night before, but he'd lost weight and there were new lines around his eyes. His grandfather's illness coupled with the search for his unborn child must have taken their toll on the man usually untouched by human frailty.

"You need to stop playing with your food and eat it."

Her head snapped up. "Don't tell me what to do."

He leaned back in his chair on the other side of the small walnut table and smiled. "It appears someone needs to. I have always heard pregnant women glow. You look as if you've just come off a nine-day flu."

Stupid tears filled her eyes. She knew she wasn't the beautiful model he'd gone to great lengths to get in his bed any longer, but did he have to rub it in? She gritted her teeth and blinked her eyes, trying to rid them of their wet sheen.

She hated the emotional weakness she'd experienced since getting pregnant. "It's a good thing I'm not trying to make a living as a model any longer then, isn't it?"

He reached across the table, grabbing her hand before she had a chance to pull it away. "I did not say you are no longer beautiful, merely that you look unwell."

She jerked her hand out from under his as the warmth of his skin burned into her own. "I'm pregnant." It was fine for him to sit there looking a bit worse for the wear, but still sexy as sin and in sickeningly good health.

"Yes, but not happily so from the look of things."

"Are you trying to imply I don't want my baby?"

He exhaled an impatient breath. "I think the fact you are five months into an obviously difficult pregnancy is ample proof you want my child."

"I don't want *your* child. I want *this* baby."

His lips creased in a devilish grin. "Same thing."

Unwilling to agree on any point, but equally unwilling to deny the truth, she remained silent and took a bite of ripe melon, savoring its sweet and juicy freshness in her mouth. "I want this baby and I'm keeping him. Do you hear me?"

His mouth twisted. "Have I at any time implied that you should not?"

"You told me you wanted my son."

"You believe I am married to Phoebe, therefore I must want the baby without the mother?" His hands lifted in an expression of exasperation she knew well. "Do I have this right?"

She wasn't totally certain any longer, so she shrugged. He could make what he liked of it.

"Your opinion of me is very low," he said grimly, all humor gone from his countenance. "I should have the proof you need of Phoebe's marriage to Spiros within the hour."

She remained mute. She'd believe it when she saw it. It wasn't his brother Spiros who had announced his engagement to the young Greek heiress.

"I can see it is of no use attempting to talk with you until I have the documents."

"I don't want to talk to you at all," she admitted.

It was a useless sentiment. She was pregnant with his child. They would have to come to terms eventually, but those terms would not include her giving up her baby.

"Do not play the child."

She forced herself to eat a bite of her eggs. Their fluffy warmth tasted like sawdust on her tongue. She had believed she was even tempered before she met Dimitri.

"You said you are no longer modeling to support yourself."

She nodded, wary of where this was leading. She

didn't want to give away any more information than she had to.

"What are you doing now?"

"Maybe I'm just living off Hunter's largess." She knew the idea of another man supporting her while she was pregnant with his child would infuriate Dimitri.

Sure enough, his eyes narrowed. "Are you?"

"I'm living with them," she pointed out.

He just waited and when she remained silent, he sighed. "I already have five reputable detective agencies on my retainer. Now that I know the name you are living under, it should be a matter of a phone call or two to elicit the information."

"I'm working as a translator and interpreter for an agency that sends out temps."

His blue eyes narrowed and his jaw tightened. "You go out to work for strangers?" He made it sound like she was some sort of call girl or something.

"It's not that different from doing a modeling assignment."

"But then you knew the photographers, the other models."

She pushed her plate aside and took a sip of herbal tea. "What difference does it make?"

"You are pregnant and obviously ill." His gaze wandered over her with tactile force. "You should not be working."

If he didn't want Hunter supporting her, how did he expect her to live? "I have to support myself. I refuse to be my younger sister's charity case."

"Why have you not returned to your parents' home?"

A traditional Greek man who shared the loving rapport he had with his grandfather could never understand the complicated relationship she had with her mother. "I'm not welcome," was all she said.

"This cannot be. You are pregnant with their grand-child. Surely your parents desire to care for you at this time."

"My father died six years ago and my mother is only willing for me to return to New Orleans and the family home if I invent a fictitious husband who conveniently died recently or lives overseas. It's positively draconian, but that's the way she is. She refuses to even discuss the baby and hasn't come to visit Madeleine since I moved in."

His jaw set. "You refused to invent this pretend spouse?"

"Yes." She'd rather live without her mother's approval than continue pretending to be something and someone she wasn't.

"It will be a relief for her then that the real and in fact living father of your child will soon be your husband as well."

CHAPTER FIVE

"As jokes go, that's not a very good one."

He fixed her with an impenetrable stare. "I am not joking, *pethi mou.*"

"Don't call me that. It's an endearment and I'm not dear to you which only makes it an insult."

He shoved his plate away from him in an uncharacteristic show of temper. "My marriage proposal is a joke and endearments an insult. Is there nothing I can do right with you?"

"You could leave me alone."

His blue eyes darkened to the color of the sky just before midnight. "This I will not do."

She forced another bite of melon down, its succulent juiciness lost on her. "I figured as much."

"Then why suggest it?"

"Wishful thinking?"

"Do not be facetious. This is a serious discussion we are having here."

"What exactly are we discussing? Your attempt at bigamy?"

His fist slammed down on the table, causing the dishes and plates to clatter alarmingly. "I am not married."

She eyed him warily, almost believing him. Maybe, deep down, she did believe him, but some imp in her wanted him to prove it, to see how it felt to have his word questioned on a claim that should be accepted without hesitation.

"So you said. Proof is to arrive within the hour, or

something like that..." She waved her hand in an airy gesture.

"Right," he gritted out between clenched teeth.

She really had to stop baiting him. "Let's say I believe you. Why would your brother marry your fiancée?"

"As I told you last night, your and my relationship came as a great shock to my family." Pain crossed his features. "The photographer did his homework and had chapter and verse on our year-long association. My brother was appalled on Phoebe's behalf. She'd been made to look a fool, something his perception of our family honor could not tolerate."

"So he married her? Wouldn't your intended marriage have been just as efficacious?"

"No. I was the philanderer, the one caught with my pants down in public so to speak."

She swallowed a smile at the imagery. Dimitri Petronides in such a vulnerable position was something she'd give a great deal to see. "I can't believe you agreed to let your fiancée marry your brother."

"He convinced her to elope with him. Her pride was saved. Our family honor was saved and now I am free to marry you."

He looked for all the world like he expected her to leap for joy and congratulate him on his good planning. She would have rather dumped his coffee in his lap. "Charming. You can marry your pregnant mistress now that the virginal bride-to-be has flown the coop. Thanks, but no thanks."

"Do you think our son will thank *you* for denying him his heritage, his Greek family, his role as my heir?"

"We don't have to be married for you to make our

son your heir or for you to be part of his life. You can have access."

"Of what good is this? You live an ocean away. How can I be his father with two continents and an ocean between us?"

"I don't know." She stood up wearily. She had to get ready to go to work. She had an assignment in two hour's time across town. "You'll have to forgive me for not having all the answers just yet. You ditched me three months ago, certain the baby I carried was not yours. I haven't been thinking in terms of parental sharing and visitation rights."

He stood as well. "Where are you going?"

"I have an assignment in a couple of hours. I'm going to get ready."

"I told you I am not allowing you out of my sight."

"Then come along," she offered sarcastically, "but I'm going to work."

She came to rue those flippantly uttered words. Dimitri insisted on doing just that. In addition, he refused to take a cab, but had his car called, along with his two bodyguards. It had been a while since she went out with security men in tow, a little over three months to be exact.

Dimitri refused to wait in the car while she did the short translation job for the group of French tourists. She walked beside the tour guide, translating the woman's rapid dialogue concerning the Empire State Building into French while Dimitri and his bodyguards brought up the rear of the line.

It would have been a comical sight if she wasn't so tired and stressed. By the time she slid into his car for the ride back to his hotel, she was disgustingly grateful she hadn't had to wait in line for a taxi. She didn't even have enough energy to enjoy looking at the city's Christmas decorations out the limousine's window. Commenting on her drooping appearance, he insisted on stopping for lunch at one of Manhattan's upscale Italian restaurants.

Alexandra walked back into the main room of the suite from her bedroom just as Dimitri was turning from the fax machine, several sheets of paper in his hand. She'd avoided him since their return by the simple expedient of taking a nap. For some reason, she'd slept better than she had in ages.

Dimitri waved the papers before her. "Proof."

"Proof?" She was still a little rummy from the nap and didn't know what he was talking about until she looked down and read the top sheet. "Oh."

She put out her hand for the sheaf of papers and he gave them to her. The first one was a marriage license. It was in Greek, but she was now almost as conversant in that language as she was in both English and French. She easily translated the names and the male listed was *Spiros* Petronides, not Dimitri.

The second one was a photo of Spiros and Phoebe in wedding regalia. Phoebe looked a little shell-shocked. Spiros looked arrogantly satisfied. Typical Petronides male.

The third was a letter from Spiros affirming Dimitri's account of the situation. This one was in English.

Alexandra took a deep breath, feeling an emotion she should not be feeling. Unadulterated relief. She told herself it was because she didn't have to worry about the complications of a stepmother being around the baby so early in life, but her heart mocked her. And that scared her to death.

"Why was she at our apartment?" She didn't notice her slip of the tongue until a look of approval settled over Dimitri's face. "I mean *your* apartment. I was evicted," she added for good measure, wiping the not fully formed smile off his face.

"I have had to take over the Athens office completely since Grandfather's first heart attack. Spiros and Phoebe moved to Paris so he could run the office there. I gave them the apartment as a wedding present."

"Is that something like conscience money? You felt guilty for embarrassing her with a public tiff with your discarded mistress, so you gave her the apartment you'd evicted me from?"

She should have kept her mouth shut. She really should have, but she couldn't seem to remember that when she was around him. His eyes snapped fury at her as he took one menacing step forward after another. She backed up, but eventually hit the wall between the main room and her bedroom.

"It was a joke," she said weakly.

"This is not."

Then his mouth closed over hers and she forgot he was only doing it to punish her. She forgot everything but how incredible it felt to be held so close to him, to taste him on her tongue, to be surrounded with his smell, his heat, his desire.

She worked her hands into the space between his jacket and his shirt, reveling in the feel of his muscles under her exploring fingers. He shuddered and she exulted in her power over this dominant Greek male. He pulled her to him, pressing their bodies as close as they could go without taking off their clothes. It wasn't close enough.

She started unbuttoning his shirt as he slid her sweater

up to expose the tight skin over her womb. His hand settled on it and he caressed her there, touching every square centimeter of the football-size lump. The baby moved and Dimitri stopped kissing her to stare down at his hand on her stomach in awe. The baby kicked right in the center of his palm and Dimitri's eyes slid shut, his breath stilling in his chest.

He let it out very slowly and met her eyes. "My son."

"Yes," she whispered, unable to deny such a poignant claim.

Triumph glowed in his indigo gaze before his mouth settled over hers again, this time with such gentleness she felt tears seep out of the corner of her eyes. He kissed her lips as if meeting them for the first time, while his hand continued to explore the new contours of her body.

His possessive touch coupled with the tenderness of his kiss completely undermined any resistance and she fell back into the kiss without a murmur.

She had his buttons undone and her fingers were circling his hardened male nipples when a shrill sound filtered through the passionate haze in her mind. She crashed back to reality with a bruising emotional bump. *What was she doing?*

She tore her mouth from his. "The phone."

His eyes were glazed with desire and his skin had that flushed look he got when they made love. He tried to catch her mouth again and she turned her head.

"The phone," she repeated as it rang again, its piercing jangle skating across her nerves.

He gently pulled the elasticized band of Alexandra's doeskin pants back to waist level before smoothing her caramel colored crocheted sweater back into place.

"This is not over," he said and then turned to answer the phone.

She walked to the other side of the suite, wanting to get as much distance between them as she could. She'd been so sure she was safe from her attraction to Dimitri, certain her feelings for him were dead. She might not love him anymore, but she wanted him and her pulsing body proved it.

"Yes, Grandfather." Dimitri went silent, apparently listening. "I remember." He cast Alexandra an assessing look. "It's being handled."

Why did she have the lowering suspicion the *it* being handled was her?

Dimitri made a few more remarks in Greek, asked his Grandfather about his health, listened silently, said goodbye and hung up. He turned to face her and she couldn't suppress a shiver. His eyes glowed like those of a predator with his prey firmly in his sights.

She stepped backward even though he hadn't made a move toward her. "That was a mistake."

He didn't ask what *that* was, he merely smiled. "I don't think so. It did not feel like a mistake to me *pethi mou.*"

"I'm not falling back into your bed, Dimitri."

"Are you certain of this?" he asked lazily.

"Yes."

"We shall see."

"I think I'll order room service. I'm hungry." Her appetite had increased over the past couple of days. Maybe the awful morning sickness was finally passing.

"I have a better idea."

"What?" she asked, feeling wary.

"Let's go out."

"I don't know…" Being seen in public with a man

of Dimitri's wealth was always a risk for media exposure.

His eyes warmed with sensual lights. "We can stay here if you prefer."

"I'll get my jacket." A woman had to know how to weigh her options and the risk of staying in the suite with a sexually charged Dimitri far outweighed her concern about being caught in his company by the media.

The muted glow of candlelight lent entirely too intimate an aspect to Alexandra's dinner with Dimitri. He'd surprised her once again by taking her to one of the *see and be seen* restaurants so popular among the sophisticated New York social set. Dim lighting didn't stop recognition and surreptitious glances from one table to another.

Alexandra tried to concentrate on the food in front of her and ignore her compelling dinner companion. Dimitri had ordered a much larger meal for her than she usually ate and she had surprised herself by consuming almost all of it. The same thing had happened at lunch that afternoon. If nothing else, sparring with her ex-lover seemed to spur her appetite.

"Xandra—"

"My name is Alexandra," she said, before he could complete his sentence. "Xandra Fortune is dead."

Something passed across his face when she made that statement, but in the dim lighting she couldn't tell if it was pain or irritation. "You had no plans to go back to modeling after the baby was born?" he asked, conspicuously using the past tense for her plans, implying she had new ones.

"No."

He studied her like a man trying to decipher a complicated puzzle. "Why?"

"There were many reasons."

"Very cryptic." He smiled in a way that used to send her pulse to hyperspeed. "Tell me some of them."

She gave a mental shrug. Why not? This at least was better than arguing over custody rights and his insulting notion that now he believed her about the baby she should fall all over herself getting to the altar before he changed his mind.

"I want to spend more time with my baby than that type of career would allow and it would be too difficult to maintain two separate lives with a baby in tow. It was hard enough for me, but I think a life like that would be confusing and probably even frightening for a child."

He mulled that over much longer than she thought necessary. "Explain to me again why the Xandra Fortune image."

Had she explained it a first time? She couldn't remember. She knew she'd alluded to it. "My mother did not approve of my working. *Dupree women do not work,*" she said in a fair imitation of her mother's soft Southern drawl. "But it was my choice of career that really upset her. The idea of her daughter traversing a catwalk in front of her peers or worse, doing swimsuit or lingerie ads sent her into hysterics."

"You chose to create a different persona rather than give up your desire to become a model?" he asked.

"I didn't have a choice. It was either pick up a career or see my mother dispossessed and my sister thrown out of boarding school for nonpayment of tuition."

"Explain this to me. Where was your father?"

"Dead."

"That is unfortunate. You have my belated condolences.'' The words were formal, but the emotion in his voice left her in no doubt to his sincerity.

"Thank you. He was a dear man, a fossil collector. Old bones interested him; business did not. Unbeknownst to the rest of us, the family had been living completely on credit for two years before he died.''

"When did this happen?''

"Six years ago. I'd just graduated from my last year at Our Lady's Bower and thankfully the cousin of a school chum had shown some interest in my modeling for his magazine.'' She took another bite of her lobster fettuccine. It practically melted in her mouth.

"Our Lady's Bower sounds like a convent, or something.''

"It is. Dupree girls have been French convent educated for the last six generations.''

"No wonder it was so easy for you to adopt a French persona. Your accent is flawless, your gestures often gallic and your outlook quite European.''

"Yes.'' She'd selected France for the debut of Xandra Fortune for those very reasons.

"Go on,'' Dimitri prompted.

She grimaced. "There's not much else to tell. Mother would have ignored the redundancy notices until the sheriff showed up to evict us from our home. Madeleine still had two years left at Our Lady's Bower and I couldn't bear for her to lose that stability after we'd all just lost Papa.''

"So you went to work.''

"Under an assumed name. I was trying to spare my mother's feelings. It didn't work.''

"She could not reconcile herself to the thought of her daughter working?''

"No.'' She smiled ruefully. "I've always felt guilty,

that I had failed her, but I simply could not think what else to do. I hadn't gone to college yet. I was too young for most well paid career choices. Modeling looked like my only option. My friend's cousin helped me create Xandra Fortune. It was cloak and dagger stuff and he really got into it. He made sure the only people who knew about Alexandra Dupree's connection to Xandra Fortune were me, my family and him."

"So this man knew you were Alexandra Dupree, but I, your lover for a year did not." He sounded mortally offended.

"Got it in one. I didn't know about Phoebe, the patiently waiting bride-to-be, either. I guess we're even on that score." Her throat felt dry from all the talking and she took a long cool sip of water.

He didn't take the bait, surprising her. "Your mother's sensibilities are the reason you refused New York assignments."

"Yes. I never took an assignment in the States period. I was careful to avoid doing commercials for international products and as you know, I tried to stay out of the media limelight in my personal life."

"Yet, you were well-known in Europe."

"Yes, but only as a French model, not a supermodel. My biggest claim to fame was being your lover and you were careful to keep that fact under wraps."

"Not completely," he said enigmatically. "You did your family a great service and your mother should be proud of you."

His words warmed her, but Alexandra felt a burble of laughter well up and let it out. "*Proud of me?* Her scandalous *working* daughter who got pregnant without the benefit of matrimony? She hadn't forgiven me yet for not saving the family home. I'll be the black sheep of the family forever at the rate I'm going.'' She tried to hide the hurt that knowledge caused her. She didn't want Dimitri to see her weakness.

"Your mother lost her home?"

"My income as a model kept my mother in Chanel suits and provided a complete education for my sister. She graduated from Smith a month before she married Hunter last year.'' Pride in Madeleine's accomplishment tinged Alexandra's voice.

Then she sighed. "The money did not stretch far enough to keep up payments on a heavily mortgaged mansion and the staff necessary to run it. Mother was forced to sell and move into a converted apartment serviced by a daily maid. Although it's still in a socially acceptable New Orleans neighborhood, it is not the Dupree Mansion.''

"And she blames you for this? Not your irresponsible father who left his wife and daughters in debt?"

She didn't take exception to Dimitri's view of her father. Dimitri was a responsible guy, someone who would never leave his family in the lurch. He couldn't comprehend a man who had absolutely no sense about money.

"Mama doesn't exactly blame me for losing the mansion, but she was furious when I wouldn't stop modeling after it was sold. She would have much preferred I married well rather than work to support her and Madeleine.''

"But you did not wish to marry well?"

"I wanted to marry a man I loved, not a bank account.''

"Then it should please you to marry me. If the words you spoke at *Chez Renée* were true, I can give you both.''

"They were true then," so much so that parts of her heart were still cracked and bleeding after the abrupt way they'd broken up, "but I don't love you anymore."

"I refuse to believe a woman of such strong character could fall out of love at the first sign of adversity."

She was beginning to have a horrible suspicion he was right, but she wasn't about to feed his smug pride admitting it. "I wouldn't call you ejecting me from your life with the force of a rocket launcher so you could marry another woman the first sign of adversity."

"Yet I did not marry her."

"Because your brother beat you to the punch."

He sighed. "You are sure I would have married her otherwise?"

Why was he asking her that? Of course she was sure. He'd made his position very clear that last meeting in Paris. "Yes."

"If I told you I had already decided not to go through with the marriage, you would not believe me, hmm?"

Was he saying that? No. This was just another one of his subtle manipulations. "Don't tax your personal integrity making the claim. You're right. I wouldn't buy it."

"And yet I had hired a detective agency to find you within days of you leaving Paris."

"I waited for you to change your mind for a whole week, Dimitri. You didn't even call. I can believe you started to consider the consequences if I'd told the truth about the baby, but I don't think you were prepared to call off your wedding because of it. *I* didn't matter to you then, and I don't matter to you now. It's all about the baby and I'm not stupid enough to forget that."

His hand gripped his wine glass very tightly. The

same hand that still wore a bandage from the night he'd come to Madeleine and Hunter's party.

"How did you cut yourself? I never asked." Her mind had been on other things that night.

He carefully put his wine glass down, staring at it as if it held the answer to an important question. Then he looked up at her and she gasped.

His eyes held a torment that was haunting.

"When Madeleine told me you were dead, I crushed the glass in my hand."

CHAPTER SIX

DIMITRI'S statement hung in the air between them like a bomb that had not exploded, but still might.

"You were that upset at the prospect of losing your child?" She had not considered Dimitri's emotional involvement with their baby. Which wasn't all that surprising considering she'd seen him as an emotionless monster for the past three months.

His jaw tautened. "If it pleases you to believe so, yes."

"I'm sorry."

He inclined his head. "With your background, you should understand the importance of our child being raised in his home country of Greece and as a Petronides."

That was more like it. Dimitri wanted his son because family pride demanded he be raised Petronides. "I understand the importance of loving my baby for his own sake, not the sake of family pride. Whether he's raised a Dupree or Petronides, he will still be worthy of my love. Can you say the same?"

Dimitri's features took on the cast of the Iceman. "Apparently you do not believe me capable of any level of emotion, so why should I bother answering?"

She'd hurt him, wounded his sense of self and for some reason, she simply couldn't bear that. "I didn't mean—"

"Leave it. Do you want dessert?"

"No." She couldn't eat anything now.

"Then we will return to the suite. If we are to have yet another argument, we will do it in privacy."

The drive back to his hotel was a silent one. She felt guilty and kept telling herself she shouldn't, but the feeling remained. Just because Dimitri did not love her did not mean he was not capable of loving his son. She'd had no right to imply that it did.

She was still trying to work up to an apology when he let them both into the suite a half an hour later.

"Dimitri, I—"

"I said leave it." He rubbed his forehead. "I'm tired."

His admission of weakness stunned her.

His lips twisted wryly. "You think I cannot get exhausted like the next man? We all have our limits, *pethi mou.*"

He hadn't in the twelve months she'd lived with him.

"I have not slept well for the three months I have searched for you," he further shocked her by admitting. "I believed once I found you, everything would fall into place. You would agree to marry me. We would be on the next plane to Greece so you could meet my grandfather. I believed I would have to assuage your anger, I did not expect to find a woman who hated me."

"I don't hate you," she averred, "I told you that."

"You do not wish to hate me for our child's sake. I understand this, but you do not want to marry me. You do not trust me. I am at a loss where to go from here. Just as you saw modeling as the only solution to your family's financial difficulties, I see marriage as the only workable solution to our situation."

It was her turn to sigh. "I know you do."

"And I am sexually frustrated." His laugh was harsh. "I don't like going without."

She didn't know if she could handle Dimitri in this strange mood. She was used to him taking charge, demanding. His admissions of weakness surprised her silly. "It hasn't been that long, surely?"

"I have not made love to another woman since the night I told you I was marrying Phoebe."

For a hopelessly oversexed male like Dimitri that was a lifetime. No wonder he wasn't himself. She didn't know why he had abstained, but something deep inside her was fiercely glad he had. "I see."

"I doubt it, but maybe you will someday." All tiredness disappeared from his expression to be replaced with predatory sensuality. "You could help me out."

She backed toward her bedroom. "I think I'll make an early night of it, t-take a shower, m-maybe read a book."

He'd already proven she couldn't resist him physically. She wasn't about to stick around and offer herself as the main course to end his months long sexual fast.

She took the image of his primitive smile with her as she closed the door to her bedroom. She pushed the lock in for good measure and took her first unhindered breath in five minutes. She couldn't let him make love to her again. She was too vulnerable to him and she needed to think. She wouldn't be able to do that with any sense of clarity while under the influence of his passionate nature.

Her eyes closed, Alexandra rinsed the lather from her hair, enjoying the feel of hot water cascading over her body from three different directions.

The luxury of the spa shower had even won out over a long soak in the oversized, jetted tub. Two showerheads shot warm showers of water toward her body from chest height while another sent down a gentle spray from above her head. She felt completely pampered in the glass and tile enclosure.

So pampered that she was almost able to push her chaotic thoughts away, but not quite. Somehow, she had to work things out with Dimitri. He had as much right to love their son as she did and more importantly, their child had a right to two loving parents if possible. Dimitri had made it clear such an eventuality was possible, *but he did not love her.*

Was it right though, for her to make her child pay the price for her own unfulfilled dreams? And their son would pay a price if she refused to marry Dimitri. He would be born outside the bonds of matrimony. For many that would not matter, but among his Greek family and future business associates, it would.

Her own mother might never accept him. While that made Alexandra furious, she knew there was little she could do to turn around a lifetime of conditioning. Her mother's belief system was as ingrained as a fossil in rock.

In his fossil research, her father had often been forced to leave rock sediment on one of his specimens because to remove it would be to destroy the fossil. She didn't want to destroy her mother. She didn't even want to upset her. Because despite her mother's irritating habit of seeing the world only from her own point of view, Alexandra loved her and wanted her to be happy.

Wishing she could brush her troubling thoughts away so easily, Alexandra swiped the water from her eyes and opened them…to blackness. She blinked, but no light penetrated the darkness surrounding her. Had there been a power outage? Didn't all the larger hotels have generators?

Suddenly the stream of water pulsing down on her head ceased. The two other showerheads kept going however, leaving her feeling disoriented. She fought down panic as she reached out to touch the tile of the wall for a sense of reference and touched bare flesh instead.

For an instant her brain could not take in the significance of the hair roughened, heated flesh under her agitated fingers. What...? Then, "Dimitri?" whispered because she couldn't force more volume from the frozen muscles in her throat.

"It is I." His voice surrounded her with more warmth than the steam from the hot water flowing over both their bodies.

"You shouldn't be here."

An arm wrapped around her waist and pulled her forward. "Should I not?" he asked against her shocked lips.

"No. I don't want this." Did she sound as unconvincing to him as she sounded to herself?

Knowing fingers brushed gently over nipples that had gone turgid and aching the moment she realized his naked body stood so close to her own. "Are you sure about that?"

"We need to talk," she tried again, while her body shook with the need to melt into his.

"No," he said with harsh emphasis. "We have talked enough. It gets us nowhere, but this..." He squeezed her nipple between thumb and forefinger and she could not stifle her moan. "This I can give you."

"Sex won't solve our problems. It's what started them

in the first place,'' she said, trying one last time to keep hold of her senses.

''*No*. It was not the sex. When we make love it is like a poem of rare beauty and beat. Words have brought this distance between us. My words. Your words. I will not let it continue. I cannot let it continue.''

The urgency in his voice affected her as deeply as the emotive words and she felt tears burn the back of her throat. He was right. Their distance had been caused by words. Making love had never been anything but beautiful between them, even that last tempestuous time.

She couldn't stand the distance any longer either, but undoubtedly for a different reason. There in the steamy darkness, she accepted a truth her heart had been telling her all along. She was not over Dimitri Petronides. She would never be over him. The love she felt for him was too strong, too deeply imbedded in her.

Again it was the fossil in the rock, only this time she knew with absolute certainty that to try to rip the love she felt for him from her breast would destroy her completely.

She made a noise of need and longing. His arm tightened around her, bringing her body flush with his own. Familiar lips closed over hers in a kiss so passionate, she felt scorched by the heat of it. Dimitri nibbled impatiently at her bottom lip until she opened her mouth and then he was inside, laying claim to her softness and reminding her of the incredible physical bond they had once shared. A bond that rejection, distance and time had not been able to sever.

Hungry for the feel of him, she let her fingers trail over the musculature of his chest. His mouth broke from hers and she sensed his head falling back as his body shuddered. "Yes, *moro mou,* touch me. I need you to touch me."

She had no hesitation about obliging him. She'd tried to hide from it, but she'd missed him so much. She circled the hard little nubs of his nipples, making him grind his already pulsingly erect flesh against her stomach.

Memories of how that flesh felt filling her would have sent her to her knees, but for the almost bruising hold he had on her waist. Running her hands up his chest and over his shoulders, she got drunk on the ability to touch him once again. She leaned forward and took one nipple into her mouth. Gently she teased it with her teeth and small flicks on the very tip with her tongue. He was moving against her with almost uncontrolled desire and she loved it.

If nothing else, she knew that in this, he was hers... completely.

She started sucking on that same erotic bit of flesh and Dimitri made hoarse sounds of need from deep in his throat. Then his hands were on either side of her face, exerting light pressure to her head. She let go of his nipple with reluctance.

"I want it to be so good for you, you will never leave me again," he vowed with a fervency that was almost frightening.

He pushed against her shoulders until she was leaning against the slick wet tile wall at the back of the square shower cubicle. "Press your hands to the wall."

She did it because she couldn't seem to stop herself.

"Do not move them."

"Dimitri?"

"Trust me."

In this, he had never hurt her and she knew deep in her heart, he never would. "All right."

Masculine fingers traced her cheeks until one brushed her lips and pressed inside. She felt warmth flood her between her legs as she sucked on that hot finger sliding in and out of her mouth. He continued the light tracing of her skin with his other hand, brushing down over her collarbone to her left breast. He stopped there, exploring her new shape brought on by changes from her pregnancy.

It was fuller and more sensitive. He seemed to sense this and kept his touch feather light as he used all five fingers in a cone motion encircling her entire breast. He brought his hand toward himself, bringing his fingers together as he did so until they circled her distended peak. He squeezed lightly and then did the entire motion all over again, and again, and again until she felt feverish with the need for his mouth on it.

"Dimitri, please... Your mouth..."

He laughed huskily. "Not yet, hmm?" Then he pulled his hand from her mouth and gave the same treatment to her other breast until her head was thrashing back and forth against the wall in an agony of need.

"Please..." She could not articulate another word.

She didn't need to. He dropped to his knees in front of her and took one straining tip into his mouth. He started off suckling ever so softly, but soon increased the pressure until the pleasure was almost pain and she was crying out.

"More, please... Oh, Heavens... Stop! I can't bear it. No... Don't stop! Harder. Now, *Dimitri!* Now..." and she came with an explosion of color in the inky blackness of their sensual prison.

She sagged against the wall, but he wasn't done. He kissed a path down to her belly. If she thought his exploration earlier of their baby's current home had been erotic, it was nothing compared to the way he caressed every new curve, every bit of skin stretched tight over her womb with both fingers and lips that almost worshipped.

"Moro mou." His baby. He kissed the center of her distended tummy. *"Yineka mou."* His woman. Both his hands covered her skin in possessive declaration.

She was so lost in her sensual daze that she almost did not catch the significance of the words whispered against the taut wall of her stomach, but when they penetrated her brain she felt emotion course through her. Earlier he had called *her* his baby, but now he was acknowledging their son. And her, but in a very different way. He'd claimed her with an endearment he'd never used with her before. Words that both connoted her place in his life as his woman, but also laid claim to her as his wife.

"I will never let you go again."

She could not respond. What could she say? He acted as if her leaving his life had been voluntary and also that it had hurt him. She didn't know if she could believe him, but she didn't have time to dwell on it. His lips were traveling down her stomach until they found her most secret place. He kissed her there, a soft salute and then exerted pressure on the outside of her thighs to bring her legs together.

She was unprepared for the penetration of his tongue. He did not pull her legs apart again, but let his tongue slide between her slick folds of femininity. He stroked her sweetest spot with the tip of his tongue, going back and forth and then in circles, all the time keeping her legs together. She couldn't believe how incredible it felt to have her inner thighs touching and the swollen flesh of her womanhood pressed together and around the wet stimulation of his tongue.

She felt the sensations of pleasure begin to build to ecstasy once again. Tears ran down her cheeks to mix with the water on her skin from the still pulsing showerheads as she said his name over and over. His hands moved from their hold on her outer thighs to cupping the underside of her bottom and she pressed herself against his marauding mouth, unable to stop the wanton movement.

Then one of his fingers penetrated where she had not been touched in over four long months and she came apart, sobbing out her pleasure and his name. He didn't stop and she bucked against him, convulsing over and over again until she went limp and the impenetrable darkness was no longer responsible for the blackness before her eyes.

She came to on the king-size bed in Dimitri's room. He was toweling her dry with gentle movements. The bedside lamp was on, casting a gentle glow over his bronzed features.

He smiled down at her. "So you have decided to wake up."

"I fainted." She couldn't believe it.

"It happens sometimes, when the feelings are very, very intense."

A surge of purely possessive jealousy coursed through her and she stiffened, glaring up at him. "I suppose you've had lots of lovers faint in your arms."

He shook his head, all trace of smile gone. "Never, *yineka mou*. Only you. Only now."

"But…" How had he known?

He shrugged as if she'd asked the question aloud. "I am a man. It is something I have heard."

"Thank you." He had given her pleasure she'd never dreamed of, not even in his arms.

His blue eyes, the color of the midnight sky, bored into her. "It is I who thanks you. I have never experienced anything like the fire you give me when I touch you."

He laid the towel across her torso, giving the illusion of modesty and straightened to stand beside the bed.

"Dimitri?"

"I will leave you to sleep in privacy if that is your wish."

She stared at him, her heart pounding in her chest. "Don't you want me?"

He laughed and flicked a self-deprecating hand in the direction of his shaft. It stood proud and pulsatingly erect out from his body. "I want you more than my next breath, but I will not take what you do not wish to give."

She would have expected him to shore up his victory in the shower with a complete seduction. In fact, she was almost sure that had been his plan. She did not know what changed his mind, but only that it touched her deeply he had. He was giving her a choice, not trying to coerce her with their physical compatibility.

And in giving her that choice, he robbed her of her resolve. She wanted him, so much. The pleasure he had given her in the shower was beautiful, something she would never forget, but she needed to feel the connection of their bodies for it to be complete.

She tugged the towel from her body and dropped it on the floor beside the bed.

His face looked hewn from stone while a wild hope burned in his indigo eyes. "Alexandra?"

She put out her arms. "I want you."

He came to her in a rush of masculine possession,

covering her body completely with his own and entering her all in one incredible move. Then he went still. "This for me is a taste of Heaven on Earth."

Alexandra strove to breathe in the face of an indescribable pleasure she'd thought never to know again. His size was such that she was stretched and filled to capacity, but her earlier pleasure had made his swift penetration easy and smooth.

She too felt a need for stillness. She wanted to savor a sensation she thought lost to her. It felt different and at first she didn't understand why, but then she remembered. He hadn't donned a condom. He hadn't needed to. She was already pregnant with his baby. She loved the feel of naked flesh against naked flesh in such an intimate way.

She tipped her head and met his gaze.

He smiled. "In this, we are in one accord."

She couldn't help returning his smile. "Yes."

Then he started to move, sliding almost completely out before entering her again with torturing slowness. "We will not hurt our son?"

She shook her head vehemently. Her obstetrician had informed her she could continue conjugal relations right up until her son's birth as long as it remained comfortable for her. She hadn't appreciated the information at the time.

She groaned as he slid in again.

"Are you certain of this?"

She forced her mind to focus so she could tell him what the doctor had said. His look of shock was so funny, she came out of her passion glazed daze enough to tease him. "You are a man. This is something you are supposed to know."

Red scorched his well defined cheekbones. "This we do not discuss."

She giggled. "I bet you didn't know that there's a chemical in your fluid that helps me go into labor when the time comes, either." That had been another helpful tidbit she'd wanted to yell at her obstetrician for sharing. She'd thought she would be spending her pregnancy alone and the prospect of getting Dimitri's *help* in this way an impossible one.

The surprised expression turned to a smug one. "A Petronides knows his duty. I will be certain to provide you all the chemicals you need at the time."

She laughed, refusing to ruin the moment by reminding either of them that she was still unsure whether or not she wanted to be in a position to allow that. Both her laughter and her disturbing thoughts melted away as he began to move more aggressively. He rocked her body with his hands while he plunged in and out of her with passionate fervor.

Incredibly she felt a tightening sensation in her lower belly, telling her that her body was preparing for another explosion of pleasure. She grabbed his shoulders, holding on so tight with her fingers that her nails dug into his skin while their bodies rocked together toward a crescendo of satisfaction.

Just as she felt herself contracting around his hardened flesh, he went absolutely stiff above her and shouted out his release. For the first time in their relationship, she was allowed to feel every pulse as his warmth flooded her and she could not believe how that impacted her emotions. It felt more intimate than anything they had ever done.

It was as if he'd always held part of himself back from her, but now he willingly gave her that which had accidentally brought about the new life in her womb. She wanted to thank him again, but the moment was too profound for words.

Whatever became of their future, she would always have this moment.

CHAPTER SEVEN

DIMITRI rolled off her, but pulled her body close to his side as if he were afraid she was going to make a break for it.

She was almost too tired to breathe. She wasn't going anywhere. "I locked the door," she murmured on a yawn against the warmth of his chest.

"Yes."

"How did you get in?"

"Do you think I only know how to make money? I can pick a lock. My grandfather's security chief taught me when I was sixteen. He said every man should have the ability. I confess it has never been of use until now."

She laughed softly, picturing a younger Dimitri learning such a questionable skill. "Did your grandfather know?"

"It was his idea."

"You're having me on."

"No. Grandfather believes a man should be able to do things for himself, even if he has the money to pay someone else to do them."

She snuggled in closer. It felt so good. "No wonder you never balked at helping me with dinner. I always thought you were surprisingly domesticated for such a traditional Greek man, not to mention such a rich one."

"I enjoyed the simplicity of our life in Paris."

"Right. You threw a fit when I told you I didn't want a live-in housekeeper, cook and maid."

"It surprised me." He defended himself. "Most

women who worked as hard as you did would have been happy to leave the domestic chores to someone else.''

"It kept me grounded. It would have been too easy to get wrapped up in the glitter and glitz surrounding the fashion industry.'' She sighed and kissed the hair roughened skin of his chest simply because she couldn't help herself. "I guess I didn't want to end up like my mother with my view of life and the world blinkered by the society surrounding me.''

But like her mother, she'd willfully worn blinders in one area of her life…with him. She had refused to *consciously* acknowledge the transitory nature of their relationship, living only in the present. So, when he ended it—she had been devastated. She didn't want to think about that right now, maybe never again.

"Why the darkness?'' she asked instead.

"I needed it to be only you and I. No more pain. No past. No present. No future. Just us.''

She understood that. Allowing this area of their relationship to be tainted by the differences that plagued them would be like taking a color marker to the Mona Lisa.

They lay like that for a long time, his fingers brushing her side in an absentminded movement while her hand rested over his heart. It reminded her of their last time together and her words then. *A strong heart.*

"You said your grandfather had another heart attack? You never told me about the first one.''

"It happened while I was in Greece that last time before you left Paris.''

"Why didn't you tell me?''

"Why didn't you tell me who you really were?'' he countered.

"I *was* Xandra Fortune in France.''

"Yes, and you took periodic trips that were not modeling assignments and yet you would not tell me what they were. Presumably they were to return to your life as Alexandra Dupree."

"Yes," she admitted.

"I thought you had met someone else."

She sat up and stared down at him, his beautiful black hair tousled by her fingers, his naked body gleaming bronze above where the sheet rested across his hips. "You thought I was two-timing you?"

Chance would be a fine thing. If he had believed that about her, he would not have stayed. "I had never had another lover. Did you think that now I knew what sex was, I couldn't wait to try it with someone else?"

She wasn't prepared for the guilty stain across his cheeks.

"You did!" She didn't think about it, she just balled up her fist and smacked him right on the chest. Hard.

He grunted and caught her hand in his own. "I did not believe it. If I had, I would have ended our relationship."

Right. That sounded like him. "But you thought the baby was someone else's."

"Yes. I did hold this tormenting belief for a week. I have no excuse."

She glared at him. "No, you don't."

But inside she had to acknowledge her trips home could have looked suspicious to a lover as possessive as Dimitri. He'd hated the fact she had things in her life she refused to tell him about. She'd kept it that way to stop him from taking her over completely. She had loved him so much, she'd needed the defense mechanism of having a part of herself he did not know. Only when she returned to living that part of her life, she took the pain of his loss with her. The defense had not worked.

"My grandfather refused to have necessary by-pass surgery until I promised to set a date for my marriage with Phoebe. I was not ready to give you up, but I was not prepared to let him die, either."

She stared at him in disbelief. "You cannot be serious. You always told me what a great guy your grandfather was. How could he blackmail you like that into ditching me?"

"He did not know about you."

This new view of what had happened three months ago left her feeling disoriented. "But still..."

"He wanted an assurance I would do my duty by the Petronides name."

"And instead you got your mistress pregnant and yourself featured in a public fight with her."

He grimaced. "Yes."

"He'll be furious if you marry me."

He looked amused. "He will be thrilled to become a great-grandfather and he cannot help but be charmed by so lovely a new granddaughter."

"I'm not beautiful anymore. You said so."

He used the grip he had on her hand to tug her down to his chest. "I said you looked ill, not ugly, you foolish woman."

"But I don't have sultry green eyes now," she said, remembering what he used to say about them.

"Now you have eyes that change color with your mood. It is quite tantalizing."

"My hair is short and mouse brown."

He laughed and tousled the aforementioned hair. "It is sexy as sin and you know it. As for the color...how can you complain when it shines like liquid sand?"

"But I'm shaped like a pumpkin."

He used one knee to part her legs so she draped across him in intimate disarray. His male hardness pressed against her. He thrust upward. "Does this feel like I think you are ugly?"

What was the question? She couldn't remember; she was too busy melting into a puddle of desire on top of him. Silence reigned while he touched her in ways she'd forgotten and brought her body to the peak of pleasure over and over again. She didn't have the energy to start another discussion when they were done. She found herself slipping into sleep cuddled against his side, feeling more at peace than she had since discovering her pregnancy.

Warm security surrounded Alexandra and she didn't want to make the trip to full wakefulness. How many times had she had this dream since leaving Paris? She was back in Dimitri's bed, his arms wrapped around her like protective bands, their lower limbs entwined to make them two parts of one whole. It seemed so real, but she knew if she allowed her mind to continue its journey toward complete lucidity, the fantasy would disappear, leaving cold reality behind.

He shifted against her, rubbing his hairy leg between her smooth limbs and she rocketed to complete wakefulness. She opened her eyes to black curling hair over a bronze, muscled chest. *Dimitri*. Along with her sensory impressions, memories of the night before blasted her conscious mind.

They had made love. Many times. He had been afraid of hurting the baby, asking her every time if it would be all right and she had reassured him. Again and again. Because she had wanted him. The last time, he'd woken her around dawn and seduced her with a sensitivity that had touched all the way to her soul.

It was incomprehensible that the man who had treated her so tenderly the night before could be the same one who had walked away from her without a backward glance.

Only according to him, he *had* looked back and found her gone. His grandfather had refused life-saving surgery until Dimitri had set a wedding date with Phoebe. While the knowledge her eviction from his life had not been voluntary soothed some of her still lacerated emotions, it did not soothe them all.

Would his grandfather have made such a demand if Dimitri had told the older man about Alexandra and implied she had an important place in his life? The problem was, she had not had that place at the time. She had been a temporary lover to Dimitri, a mistress to an unmarried man.

Last night had not felt like the joining of a man and his temporary lover or mistress, though. It had felt almost sacred.

Knowing about his grandfather put a new perspective on the events four months ago, but the older man wasn't the reason Dimitri had denied paternity of their baby. As much as she didn't want to, she had to take some of the blame for that one. By withholding part of her life from him, she had set up fertile ground for distrust to grow.

In some ways, Dimitri had done the same to her. He hadn't told her about his grandfather's heart attack and when she asked about his family, he had been reticent. She knew things about his brother and his grandfather, but he'd always changed the subject when his parents came up. They hadn't died until he was ten, so it couldn't be because he had no memories of them. He'd never taken her to meet his family, never invited his brother to the apartment for a meal when the younger man was in Paris.

Now he wanted her to marry him. She shifted restlessly, at once both loving and hating the sense of security his warmth provided. What had changed? *The answer to that was obvious,* she derided herself. One, she was pregnant with a baby he now accepted he had fathered. For a Petronides male, that would change a lot. Hadn't she known that when she told him?

At the time she had hoped it would have the exact result it finally had: his desire to marry her. Now that desire felt like too little too late.

The second change was that his wife-to-be had married his brother. Dimitri had acted like the betrayal hadn't mattered to him, but even if his emotions had not been involved…his pride would have been. A quick marriage of his own would assuage some of the wounds his pride had sustained, particularly if it was to a woman who had adored him like she once had done.

She'd recognized last night that she still loved him, but she didn't *adore* him. Did that make her any less vulnerable?

"Have you figured it all out yet?" Dimitri asked from above her head.

She tilted back to look him in the face. "Figured what out?"

"Your life. My life. Our life together."

"What makes you so sure I was thinking about us? Or that I was thinking at all, for that matter?"

His smile was grim. "As much as you may want to deny it, I know you, *pethi mou.* You often spend your first waking moments lost in thought and what is of more importance to you at the moment than the future of the baby you carry?"

"You assume that future has to include you."

"You know it does. Married or not, lovers or enemies, whatever relationship you and I share, I will have a part in my son's life."

She didn't balk at the implacability in his voice. She hadn't meant to imply otherwise. Her wording had been unfortunate. "I didn't mean that. I will not withhold your child from you."

"No matter how much you despise me?" His voice was bleak and his face expressionless.

She stared at him. Could he honestly believe she despised him after the way she had responded to him last night? "I don't despise you."

"But you no longer love me."

To answer would require a lie, so she sidestepped. "Did you have plans for today?"

"Yes."

"Then, I guess we'd better get up."

He smiled wickedly down at her. "Not necessarily."

"But…"

"My plans today are to woo you. I think here," he said, indicating the bed, "is where I am at my best."

She didn't know what she would have said because at that precise moment, the phone rang. Giving her a last lascivious look that made her giggle despite her heavy thoughts, he turned to answer the bedside phone.

Was he really going to woo her? The thought was tantalizing. She remembered his two-month-long pursuit before he'd seduced her into bed and talked her into moving in with him. They had been heady days. Living with him had been pretty wonderful too, but a wooing…well, it sounded nice.

"Alexandra."

She looked up from her blind contemplation of his naked back. "Hmm?"

"The phone is for you. It is your sister."

Alexandra crawled across the bed and took the phone from Dimitri's outstretched hand. "Madeleine?"

"Yes. It's me. How are things going with you-know-who?" Madeleine sounded nervous.

"Don't ask."

"That bad, huh?"

Bad? No. More like foolish. Falling into bed with Dimitri the first time around hadn't been her smartest move, but doing it this time, when their future was unsettled and she was still dealing with the effects of his betrayal was outright stupidity. "We've got a lot to discuss, that's all."

"Did he show you proof he didn't marry that Greek girl?"

"Yes."

"That's good anyway. Hunter said he would. Maybe he's not a complete swine."

"Hunter or Dimitri?" she asked facetiously.

"Both," was her sister's surprising and emphatic reply.

"Is everything all right, *chérie?*"

"Well…"

"Madeleine…" she said in a voice she had used since childhood to encourage her sister to *fess up*.

"It's all Hunter's fault!"

Hunter, the man who went to any lengths to make her sister happy? Alexandra had a hard time believing he'd done anything to hurt Madeleine. "What's all his fault?"

"He had a business contact invite Dimitri to the party...on purpose!"

Pure shock traveled through Alexandra. *"What?"*

"He said he was worried about you. He didn't think you were adjusting to life without Dimitri very well and wanted to know if there was a chance for you two. Hunter made discreet inquiries and found out Dimitri had been searching for Xandra Fortune since a couple of days after you landed in New York. Remember that time he suggested you call Dimitri and try to work it out?"

She remembered. It had been a week after the ultrasound. "I told him I'd rather move in with Mama."

Madeleine laughed, albeit stiltedly. "He didn't know you thought Dimitri was married and he couldn't figure out why you wouldn't at least give the father of your baby one more chance."

"So he decided to take the choice out of my hands?" she asked, feeling both outraged and outclassed. Hunter had been right and she and Dimitri did need to work out their future, whatever that might be. Still... "Save me from arrogant men."

"I slept in the guest room," Madeleine said with a certain amount of satisfaction.

Evidently Hunter didn't know how to pick a lock.

"I'm sorry, Maddy. I don't want you and Hunter arguing because of me."

"He could have told me his plans. I might even have gone along if he told me Dimitri wasn't really married."

"Maddy!"

"Well, Hunter was right about one thing. You were wilting without Dimitri. You sound more alive this morning than you have in the past three months."

Alexandra didn't know how to respond to that bit of

truth, so she changed the subject. "Is that all you called about?"

"Actually, no…" She was back to sounding nervous. What more could there be?

"Mother flew in on an early morning flight and she wanted to know where you were and I didn't want to tell her, but then Hunter came in. And just like a man, he didn't realize he'd be starting World War III and told her you were staying at a hotel with Dimitri. Mother fainted and I screamed at Hunter and now *he's* not speaking to *me*…" At this point Madeleine's voice broke.

"Oh, *chérie*. I don't want my problems to become yours."

Madeleine gave a watery laugh. "That's so like you. You took care of mother and me when Daddy died and tolerated Mama's disapproval. But when it comes time to lean on someone else, you feel guilty, for Heaven's sake!"

"I got myself into this mess. No one else should have to pay the price for my stupidity."

Dimitri stiffened beside her.

"Well, Mama's on her way over to get you out of it!"

She couldn't have heard right. "But…"

"She threatened to swoon again like some Victorian maiden, but the thing is, she looked pale as death…so I told her what hotel Dimitri was staying in and your room number."

Madeleine started crying and saying she was sorry over and over again. Her argument with Hunter and having their mother descend on her had clearly taken its toll.

"Calm down, Maddy. It will be fine. She's my

mother, of course I don't mind you telling her where I am," Alexandra said, lying through her teeth.

"But the newspapers. They're awful. I don't know how you're going to handle it."

Newspapers? "What are you talking about, Maddy?"

"You don't know?" Madeleine started crying again. "It's just terrible and after all you've been through already."

Knowing she wasn't going to get another coherent word out of her sister, Alexandra did her best to calm Madeleine before hanging up the phone. She turned to face Dimitri. "My mother is on her way over."

Dimitri's brow rose. "So I gathered."

"She's on the warpath, though Mother's version of warfare is quite genteel." That had never stopped Alexandra from feeling like she'd been through the meat grinder after one of her mother's lectures though.

"She is your mother. Her greatest concern is for your welfare," he said with absolute confidence.

She just laughed, although the sound was a hollow one. "Mama's highest priority is the dignity attached to the Dupree name. Appearance is everything and my staying in your suite doesn't look right no matter how you wrap it up and tie it with a pretty little bow."

He was silent for several seconds, his regard so intent, she felt heat rush into her cheeks. "What?" she finally demanded.

"I am shocked at my own naiveté. I believed the whole Xandra Fortune image. A French fashion model, an orphan, a woman of the world with a sophisticated outlook on life, a woman who had no sense of family responsibility because she'd never had one."

"And?" Honestly, some times talking to him was like going through a maze blindfolded and tipsy from too much wine. What was his point? And what did all this have to do with the impending visit from her mother?

He shook his head as if clearing it. "Many things did not fit the image if I had but looked at them."

"You were interested in an uncomplicated relationship with a worldly model. You saw what you wanted to see."

"This is true." He reached out and touched her cheek in an oddly affectionate gesture. "It is also true I saw what you wanted me to see, hmm?"

She couldn't deny it. She had considered telling him the truth of her background so many times, but self-protection had kept her silent. And then there had been the fear that he would lose interest in the real Alexandra Dupree. It had been a big enough shock that a man like Dimitri could find her Xandra Fortune persona desirable.

"Well, you know what they say… You don't usually know people as well as you think you do." She could admit now that both she and Dimitri were guilty of that truth.

"But you made it a point to prevent me from knowing you."

That wasn't strictly true. "You knew me, the woman. I only hid the trappings of my life as Alexandra Dupree."

"And gave me a false set of realities to replace them."

"In a way, you are a lot like my mother. You only see the surface. You only want the surface," she declared.

He tugged her into his arms and brushed his warm hand over the slope of her breast. Her nipple, still sensitive from their loving the night before, went erect immediately.

"It is true I like this surface." His smile was pure seduction, but then he went serious. "It is not all I desire, however. I want all of you and I will have all of you."

The possessive determination in the words made her shiver. She had the awful feeling he didn't just mean marriage. He wanted her mind and her emotions. It was there in his eyes and he would settle for nothing less.

"Madeleine said something about a newspaper, but wouldn't give me the details. I think you'd better look into it. Someone may have seen us together and is now speculating on who the billionaire's pregnant companion is."

He didn't look worried. "After we shower I will make a phone call."

She nodded and tried to pull away. "Mother's already left Madeleine's. She'll be here in less than thirty minutes unless she hits traffic. We need to get showered and dressed."

He stopped her from hopping out of bed. "Things have changed for us, have they not?"

"Because we had sex?"

He leaned down and kissed her on the tip of her nose. "Because we have once again established an area of our relationship that is nothing but beautiful."

"I won't let you seduce me into marriage," she said vehemently.

"Are you sure about that?" he asked, his wandering hands now wreaking havoc with her breathing.

She didn't answer and he laughed, pulling her from the bed toward the shower. "Come, we will bathe together and save time."

CHAPTER EIGHT

ALEXANDRA had been worried Dimitri would try to make love to her in the shower again, but he was as good as his word. They were dressed in record time and Dimitri was on the phone to his assistant when a gentle *rat-a-tat-tat* sounded on the door.

"Mother," she breathed.

Dimitri turned from the phone and gave her a sharp look. He cut the connection abruptly and crossed the room to open the door. Cecelia Dupree stood on the other side, looking fragile and quite lovely in her pale pink Moschino suit.

"You must be Xandra's mother," Dimitri said as he led Cecelia through the door.

Alexandra had to stifle a groan at his slip of the tongue. Her mother's face pinched and she swung on Alexandra, for once forgetting the social niceties. "So, this is what you do when you're living high as Xandra Fortune. Have you no sense of decorum at all? You're in New York now, where you are known as Alexandra Dupree. What do you think New Orleans society will say when they discover you've spent the night with some foreigner in his hotel room?" she asked in an outraged voice. "Think of your sister. The scandal could adversely affect Hunter's business dealings."

"I sincerely doubt Hunter's business associates care one way or the other about the behavior of Madeleine's pregnant sister, as for New Orleans society…I'm not taking out an ad in the paper. Why should anyone back home know?'' Or care, she asked herself silently. Her mother lived in such a rarified milieu, she didn't know how ninety percent of the world thought and functioned.

"You are a Dupree,'' her mother said as if that should explain it all. "Yet, by the look of this,'' she said, waving a newspaper in Alexandra's face, "you have completely forgotten that fact. How could you allow this sort of information to become public knowledge?''

Alexandra put her hand out toward Cecelia. "May I see, Mama? The accused has a right to know the charges.''

Cecelia flung the paper toward Alexandra with an absolutely surprising lack of restraint. When Alexandra saw the headline and pictures, she understood why. One picture was of her and Dimitri leaving the restaurant they'd had lunch in yesterday. The other was of her and Dimitri yelling at each other at *Chez Renée*. The headline read, "Greek Tycoon and Lover Reunite: Does Petronides Now Believe the Baby is His?''

With a sense of impending dread, Alexandra read the article. She was named as the famous French model Xandra Fortune *and* the *quiet living* Alexandra Dupree. The writer speculated as to the reason for her dual personas and the effect her pregnancy had had on Dimitri's scuffed plans to marry Phoebe Leonides. Dimitri's denial that he was the father was quoted, apparently having been overheard by the enterprising photographer or someone who'd been with him.

The writer went on to say it appeared Dimitri now accepted his role as father and ended the article with a pithy comment regarding a possible marriage between them.

Alexandra felt sick and she made a mad dash for the bathroom. When she finished retching, Dimitri was there with a cold wet washcloth for her face and a glass of water to rinse her mouth. When she was done, he swung her into his arms and carried her back into the main room of the suite. He set her gently on the cream colored sofa.

"I'm going to order some food, all right *moro mou?*"

She couldn't take it in. She couldn't even look at her mother, knowing how furious and disappointed in her Cecelia was bound to be. She'd spent years living two lives to protect her mother from embarrassment and possible scandal, only to have it all torn apart with one sleazy newspaper article. "Dimitri, they know… Everyone knows about us, about the baby, about Xandra Fortune."

He laid his finger against her lips. "Shh. All will be well. You must trust me. Now what do you want to eat?"

"Dry toast and maybe a little fruit."

He shook his head, his expression wry. "That is not sufficient sustenance for you and the baby. I will order your dry toast, fruit and some food besides, I think."

"Why ask me if you plan to do what you want anyway?" she asked petulantly, glad to focus on something less volatile and damaging than the newspaper article.

He chuckled. "Perhaps because I like to hear your voice?"

Her mother gave a most unladylike snort, reminding both Dimitri and Alexandra she was there.

Dimitri turned to Cecelia. "I understand your concern and will do everything in my power to mitigate it, but I will not allow you to harangue your daughter. She is in too fragile a state right now."

"How dare you?" her mother demanded.

"Can I order anything for you?" Dimitri asked, ignoring her mother's outraged question.

Apparently realizing when she was faced with a will stronger than her own, Cecelia subsided. She took a seat in one of the armchairs opposite the couch, her expression dour. "Tea might settle my nerves."

"Then I shall order you some without delay."

He went to the phone to do so, but kept his body toward them as if he were watching her mother to make sure she said nothing to upset Alexandra. His concern felt nice and Alexandra had to admit she was glad she wasn't alone to face her mother's recriminations. When he finished making the order, Dimitri returned to sit next to Alexandra on the smallish sofa. He took her hand and squeezed it reassuringly then turned the full force of his charm on her mother.

"Mrs. Dupree, allow me to introduce myself. I am Dimitri Petronides." His smile would have melted stone. He stood and leaned toward Cecelia, extending his hand. "It is an honor to meet the mother of the woman I intend to marry."

Alexandra sucked in air so fast she choked on it while her mother's "just sucked on a lemon" look turned to calculated charm in the space of a single heartbeat. Cecelia patted her perfectly coiffed ash-blond hair and smiled at Dimitri.

"Please, you must call me Cecelia. Marriage will be just the thing to alleviate the scandal. I'm so glad you'd already thought of it. Alexandra's been so impetuous these past six years and I declare the last three months have been the *worst*."

Alexandra gritted her teeth at her mother's digs. "I haven't agreed to marry him."

Cecilia dismissed Alexandra's words with a wave of

her hand. "Of course you will, dear. Now let's start making plans. It will have to be a quiet affair if there's any hope of avoiding more scandal."

Alexandra hadn't told her mother anything about Dimitri, including the details of their breakup. But she doubted it would have made any difference in the older woman's current outlook. In Cecelia Dupree's mind, babies came after marriage. Therefore, to preserve appearances, Alexandra had to be married.

"This isn't the Middle Ages, Mother. You cannot give my hand in marriage to a man without my permission." She turned her head to meet Dimitri's eyes. "And *you* can't *take* it."

"Alexandra, is that reporter correct? Is this man the father of your child?"

Alexandra's vocal chords froze. An affirmative answer would be her downfall with her mother.

"Yes," Dimitri said when Alexandra refused to.

"Then there can be no question that you will marry him."

"On the contrary." Alexandra didn't like the feeling of pressure emanating from both her mother and Dimitri. "I'm perfectly capable of having this baby alone. If that upsets you, I'm sorry."

She was proud of her little speech until her mother's eyes filled with tears. "Wasn't six years spent worried someone would discover my daughter's lifestyle enough a cross to bear? Now everyone *knows*." She sniffed and Alexandra felt a tug on her own emotions even though she suspected the tears were a tool as well used as her mother's Southern charm. "Now you balk at making things right. Think of the baby," was Cecelia last emotive appeal.

"You say lifestyle like my being a model was the

same as selling my favors to the highest bidder."
Alexandra was more comfortable on the familiar ground
of arguing her career choice rather than her current predicament.

Her mother shuddered. "How can you say such a
thing? To even imply..." Clearly words failed her and
two tears spilled over to trail down her powdered cheeks.

Alexandra felt the familiar sense of failure well up in
her. "I'm sorry, Mother. I shouldn't have said it."

Her mother dabbed at her eyes with a perfectly white,
lace trimmed handkerchief and simply shook her head
in mute disapproval.

Knowing there would be nothing accomplished by
sticking with the current subject, Alexandra asked,
"What are you doing in New York, Mother?"

The paper with the damaging story had only come out
that morning, not enough time for her mother to have
made the trip from New Orleans unless she had already
planned it.

Her mother sniffed and turned appealing eyes to
Dimitri. "I'd come north to try and talk some sense into
Alexandra, to mend fences before Christmas. A family
should spend the holidays together, don't you think? But
she's been so stubborn about her unfortunate circumstance, refusing to do anything practical to diminish the
scandal. And here she is again, refusing to marry you.
Is it any wonder I'm almost ill with my worries?"

"I do not consider the conception of my child an unfortunate circumstance," Dimitri replied in freezing
tones. "I also fail to see why the fact your daughter
modeled under the name of Xandra Fortune is such a
tragedy for you. From what she has said, her work sup-
ported both you and your younger daughter for several
years."

My, my. When Dimitri decided to defend someone, he came out with both guns blazing.

"But she didn't just model did she? She was your mistress, a tycoon's plaything," Cecelia said, quoting the article. "Now she is pregnant with your child. The Duprees have never had so much scandal attached to their name. What the nuns would think, I have no idea. Why, I'm terrified to send my monthly letter to Mother Superior for fear of letting something slip."

"Nuns?" Dimitri asked.

"The convent, remember?" Alexandra whispered.

"Ahh...those nuns."

Cecelia said, "Mother Superior didn't approve of the Xandra Fortune debacle any more than I did."

The unfairness of her mother's constant disapproval cracked something open in Alexandra. "My life as a model was hardly a debacle. Dimitri's right. It kept you in designer dresses and Madeleine in school. If I hadn't created Xandra Fortune, how would we all have lived? I can't see you getting a job."

Her mother gasped.

Someone knocked on the door. It turned out to be room service and Dimitri insisted Alexandra eat before the conversation was resumed. Her mother drank her tea with an expression of martyred stoicism.

When they were done and Dimitri had called to have the dishes removed, he resumed his seat beside Alexandra. Putting an arm around her waist, he met her mother's gaze. "Let me make a couple of things clear. One, I intend to marry your daughter. And two, it will not be some hole in the corner affair not befitting the bride of a Petronides."

He ignored both her and her mother's outraged gasps and stood.

"I'm glad you took the time to come by and see us," he said, taking her mother's arm and gently lifting her from the chair before he guided her to the door, "but as I'm sure you are aware, Alexandra and I have a great deal to do before the wedding. Perhaps we can get together this evening or tomorrow to discuss plans."

He continued talking as if he had both her and her mother's complete cooperation as he led Cecelia from the suite.

Dimitri called for his car and waited in the hotel lobby with Cecelia until it came. He shook his head watching Cecelia walk regally from the hotel. Running interference for Alexandra with her mother was going to take vigilance. Cecelia had tried to convince him again to consider a modest wedding by saying it would be cruel to Alexandra to make a media event of it when she had so obviously anticipated her wedding vows.

The car had not arrived one moment too soon.

Dimitri stepped into an empty elevator and pressed the button for his floor.

Would Alexandra be ashamed to marry him while she was so visibly pregnant? He thought back to what he had learned of her past. She'd been educated by nuns. Hell, maybe she would be embarrassed by a big wedding.

She had certainly been upset about the news clipping. He didn't want her upset and the part he had played in the breaking of the news story troubled him. He'd seen one of the paparazzi that often followed him outside the restaurant where they had eaten lunch. He hadn't said anything, had not sent his security man after the film—though as he'd learned in the past, that move was not always successful. His actions could be considered ruthless, but he thought of them as the acts of a desperate man.

She had to marry him.

For her own sake because she needed him.

For the baby's sake because he was a Petronides.

For Dimitri's sake because he needed her.

And for the sake of a promise he had made to his grandfather, a second promise when the first had been nullified.

He'd thought it would be easy once he found her. She'd obviously wanted marriage before she left Paris, but now she acted like the thought of it was worse than spending the rest of her life in Purgatory. No matter what she said to the contrary, it was obvious she now hated him. He mourned the warmth that used to shine from her eyes when she looked at him. The smile that had been just for him. Intimate. Special. He'd taken her for granted when he had her. He had ignored the underlying emotional commitment in their relationship.

He'd believed they had no hope of a future.

She'd been a career fashion model. It was lowering to admit, but he'd believed she had every intention of moving on when her career took off. He hadn't known about her family, hadn't realized she had no desire to be a supermodel. That ignorance had cost him three months of mental anguish wondering where she was and how she was faring with her pregnancy.

He'd never once considered she might terminate it…even when he'd gone to the apartment in Paris a week after she left and found her message for him on the floor of the living room.

She'd rejected everything he'd ever given her down to the sexy nightwear he'd bought her. His fists clenched at his sides when he thought of that neatly folded stack of silk and lace garments. He'd taken one look at the pregnancy test sitting on top and driven his fist through the wall. One look. That was all it had taken for him to realize she'd been telling him the truth. He hadn't understood how it could be true, but he had *known* it was.

He'd called the detective agency that very night, but it had still been too late. He'd lost her.

He'd spent three months tormenting himself with if-only scenarios. If only he had been thinking more clearly when his grandfather delivered his ultimatum, but Dimitri had been badly shaken and had gone into damage control mode. He would do anything to save his grandfather and he had done, hurting both himself and Alexandra in the process.

If only he had believed her about the baby from the beginning and told his grandfather then.

If only he had come back to the apartment sooner, but he hadn't been able to face its emptiness, the reality of what he had done to his woman. He hadn't been able to stay in Athens either, not after the announcement of his marriage to Phoebe had been made.

Everything had felt wrong about it. He'd seen the looks his brother gave Phoebe when he thought no one noticed. Dimitri could not miss the way Phoebe stood in fearful awe of him, but laughed in his brother's company. But most importantly—the look on Alexandra's face when he'd denied her haunted him.

He deserved her hatred, but he couldn't live with it. He had to convince her to marry him. He could not consider the alternative. She and the baby needed him even if she refused to admit it. *Theos* knew he needed her. Would she ever look at him with the warmth of affection in her beautiful eyes again?

*   *   *

Alexandra had picked up the paper her mother left behind and was rereading the article about her and Dimitri when he returned.

She looked up. "I can't believe they said all this. It's horrible. Conjecture about our relationship, your reasons for denying paternity. Where did all this come from?"

Dimitri shrugged. "The story ran for weeks in France and Greece, even some London papers picked it up. The press release your agency sent out saying you had retired from modeling and wanted to live a more anonymous life was all the more scintillating when news of your possible pregnancy got out. I'm surprised you didn't see any of the stories."

She'd avoided the European scandal rags after the announcement of his marriage to Phoebe. Alexandra hadn't wanted to see any pictures of the couple together. And of course, the stories hadn't made it to the States. They were about a French fashion model and a Greek tycoon, nothing of interest for American readers. At least not until the connection to her real identity was made.

"How did they make the connection?" she wondered aloud.

"I am, unfortunately, followed by a certain amount of paparazzi wherever I go. Once we were seen together, it was only a matter of time before one of them recognized you."

"But no one else had," she said helplessly.

"I find that inexplicable."

A wavery smile tilted her lips. "You certainly weren't fooled."

Remembered anger shimmered in his eyes. "No."

"You were so sure it was me and yet I must have looked very different to you," she mused.

"You are my woman. I would recognize you in the dark."

"You did," she said, helplessly remembering the passion they'd shared the night before.

His smile was predatory. "Yes."

"Sex isn't everything," she admonished him.

"But it is a start, is it not, *yineka mou?*" He resumed his seat beside her and placed his hand against her protruding belly. "And we have this precious child we share as well."

If only she could believe him, but she didn't trust him. Did he have an ulterior motive for the marriage? "You're afraid I won't give you access, aren't you? You think you'll have more say in our baby's life if we're married."

"I will, but that is not why I want to marry you."

"Then why?" she demanded.

"You once said we had something special. Perhaps I want that back again."

"Impossible."

"Nothing is impossible, Alexandra."

Believing he might come to love her was. "I don't know," she said, achingly aware her desires were at odds with her intellect. She wanted to marry him, but she was afraid doing so would only open her heart to more hurt.

"Your mother will be devastated if you refuse me."

Alexandra knew that all too well. "My mother's feelings do not dictate my life."

"You can say that after spending six years living a double life to protect her sensibilities?"

"Living as Xandra Fortune was infinitely preferable to the prospect of living as Alexandra Petronides." She didn't know why she'd said it. To wound him as he had once wounded her? Regardless, guilt assailed her the second the words left her.

His jaw tautened, his blue eyes flashing anger. "Think of our child. Life as a legitimate Petronides will be *infinitely preferable* to life as the bastard child of the black sheep of the Dupree family," he said, throwing her words back at her.

She flinched with the pain the words inflicted. "Don't use that word!"

His face registered regret and then determination. "I will never use it again in relation to our son, regardless of your decision, but I cannot say the same for others."

"I know." She felt tears fill her eyes and she tried to blink them away.

He cursed in Greek and pulled her against his chest. "Do not cry, *pethi mou.* I cannot stand it."

"Then it's a good thing you weren't around for the first month after I left Paris. I did nothing but cry," she said, hiccuping with her swallowed tears.

His arms tightened around her until she squeaked from the pressure. He loosened his grip immediately. "I did not intend to hurt you."

Was he talking about just now, or three months ago? She looked at him. "Tell me about your parents, Dimitri. You never have."

His sensual lips thinned.

"How can you expect me to marry you when you won't share your family with me? I've never even met your grandfather or your brother."

"I will invite my brother to the wedding, unfortunately Grandfather cannot travel yet. You will meet him when we go to Greece."

"What do you mean, go to Greece?"

"It is where we will live."

"What if I want to live in New York?"

"Do you?" he asked with more patience than she expected.

She met his gaze and then looked away. "I don't want to raise our son in a big city," she admitted, knowing she was playing right into his hands.

"This is good." He gently tugged her face back around so she was caught in the compelling blue of his gaze. "The family home is on a small island off the coast near Athens. There is nothing on the island but the Petronides home and a fishing village. It will be a wonderful place for our son to grow up. I should know. I was raised there."

It sounded all too tempting.

CHAPTER NINE

"IF I marry you and you divorce me, you could keep my baby," she said, expressing her deepest fear.

He swore and stood. "You believe I would do this to you?"

She wanted to deny it. He looked so angry. "I don't know. I don't trust my instincts where you are concerned anymore."

"Marriage is forever. I would not do this." She could tell it infuriated him to have to say it. His pride was wounded and for some reason that made her feel bad. "This baby and the ones to come after will have both their mother and their father to raise them."

"You want more children?" The thought had never occurred to her.

"Yes. Do not tell me you only want this baby?" The thought clearly horrified him.

"No. I want at least two, but would really like four."

"Don't you think you had better marry me beforehand?"

"For the baby's sake?" she asked, wishing it could be different.

"For his sake yes, but also for your sake."

"You mean I won't have to work to support us both if I marry you?"

"You would not have to work regardless. From this point forward, you and the baby are my responsibility."

"Thank you." She knew he meant what he said. It

was written on the immovable features of his gorgeous face.

"You will be happier married to me than as a single parent," he asserted with inbred arrogance.

"You think so?"

"I know this."

"How can you be so certain?"

"Whatever you need to make you happy, I will give it to you."

Everything but his love, she thought sadly. But she would have his passion. Last night had proven that. She would have his support. He'd given her a taste of it this morning with her mother and it had been sweet. She would have his respect. If he did not respect her, he wouldn't be asking for marriage, she was sure of it.

"It would certainly relieve my mother's mind."

A calculating expression entered his eyes. "If you marry me, I will buy back the Dupree Mansion and staff it with servants for your mother's lifetime."

The sheer generosity of the offer stunned her. She understood his willingness to provide for her and the baby, but to take on responsibility for her mother as well was excessive and very, very endearing.

"Mama would love you forever."

"Yes." He frowned. "She does not want a big wedding. She believes you would be embarrassed. Is she right?"

"Embarrassed? To be marrying you?" she asked incredulously.

"To be married publicly when you are so obviously *enceinte*."

"I'm not ashamed of my baby." She wasn't comfortable with the fact he'd been conceived in a relationship rather than a marriage, but her son was precious to her all the same.

Dimitri's expression lightened. "I am very proud that you carry my child, *yineka mou.*"

Alexandra pictured a traditional wedding, she and Dimitri decked out in formal white, her veil and train brushing the floor at least three feet behind her.

"Your eyes have gone soft and golden. Of what do you think, little one?"

She felt herself blushing, but decided to tell him. "I know it sounds really naff, but I always wanted to wear a traditional white wedding dress with a long train and oodles of lace in my veil." She sighed and touched her tummy. "But then I guess I would look pretty silly in white in my state."

He returned to the sofa and took her hand in his. "White is the sign of a pure heart. You would not look silly to me."

Her breath caught and she had to concentrate on getting her lungs to expand again. "I wouldn't?"

He leaned forward and she closed her eyes in preparation for his kiss. Why didn't she have more self-control with him? She felt a touch so light it almost wasn't there on both her eyelids, her cheeks and finally her lips. They parted of their own accord and the pressure increased.

He ended the kiss scant seconds later, leaving her feeling dazed.

That was nice.

He laughed and she realized she'd spoken aloud.

She smiled at him. "So you think I should wear white?"

"Yes."

"I'd like that."

"Does this mean you will marry me?"

Had there ever really been any doubt? Because she didn't want her pride stomped in the dust, she said, "It's the best thing for the baby."

His tender expression turned to stone and he stood up quickly from the sofa. "There are plans to be made. I want to be married a week from today."

"So quickly? What about my dress, the church—"

"I will take care of it."

She didn't argue. She supposed a billionaire could pull together a wedding on nothing notice. Money talked, or so they said. "I'm picking out my own dress."

He shrugged. "As you like."

He turned toward the phone, all signs of his loverlike countenance gone.

"Dimitri?"

He pivoted to face her. "Yes?"

"This is what you want?"

He laughed harshly. "I am getting what I deserve and can expect nothing more."

"But I thought you wanted to get married." Had she completely misread the situation? The one hope she clung to was the knowledge that he wanted her. Had last night satisfied that craving?

"I do." His eyes blazed certainty at her.

"But you seem unhappy now that I've said yes."

He came back and pulled her up and into his arms. "I am not unhappy, *pethi mou*. I am merely preoccupied with the details of the wedding now that you have agreed."

It made sense and she had no fears while his arms were around her. She yawned. "All right."

He turned her toward the bedroom and patted her bottom gently. "Take a nap. Pregnant ladies need their rest."

She went, feeling comforted. He'd pointed her in the direction of his bedroom. It was only later, while she hung on the verge of sleep that she realized he had once again sidestepped the issue of his parents.

Dimitri gripped the phone tightly without dialing. What had he expected, that she would say she was marrying him because she wanted to? At least she had agreed. He should not bemoan the fact it had been for the child's sake alone.

He would convince her to trust him again. He would show her that what they had had in Paris could be theirs again. The affection. The fun. The rapport. And once she saw that he would never dismiss her so cruelly again, she would once again glow in his presence.

At least he'd kept *this* promise to his grandfather.

"You are nervous, *yineka mou*. Why?"

Alexandra shifted the yards of fabric in her wedding dress's skirt an inch to the left on the limousine's seat. "There are going to be a lot people at the reception."

Which was an understatement. Dimitri had managed to invite an obscene number of wedding guests, all of whom would be staying for the reception...including Dimitri's brother, Spiros, and his wife Phoebe.

"You have modeled swimwear in front of a bigger crowd."

True. But the crowd had never included Dimitri's ex-fiancée and brother. "Does Spiros think I'm an awful tramp?"

Dimitri reeled as if she'd struck him and his eyes burned angry blue fire. "Why should you think this? Do you feel like this marriage has made you one?"

She wondered how Dimitri managed the Petronides

Corporation so effectively with his lousy communication skills. "Of course I don't feel like a tramp because I married you. It's just that your brother's read those awful articles. I'm sure he blames me for Phoebe's humiliation."

"My brother does not blame you."

She waved Dimitri's words aside. "Don't be ridiculous. Who else would he blame? I was the *other woman* even if I didn't know it. He had to marry Phoebe to save the family honor. I bet he hates me," she wailed.

Dimitri pulled her onto his lap, yards of white satin and all. He took her chin in his hand and forced her to look at him. "My brother does not blame you. He knows you were unaware of Phoebe's existence. He knows where the real blame lies. With me."

"But he's your brother. He's bound to forgive you." Look how many times she forgave Mama. "He's free to hate me." Dimitri laughed. He actually laughed and she wanted to sock him. "It's not funny. Your family's got no choice but to think you've married some kind of opportunist, five months pregnant with your baby and they've never met me."

"Spiros and my grandfather know this too is my fault. Do not worry, Alexandra. Spiros is content in his marriage and excited at the prospect of being an uncle. You made both things possible. He will adore you."

She would have continued her lament, but the limousine slid to a smooth stop and seconds later the door opened. Dimitri lifted her in his arms.

She squealed. "You're supposed to carry me over the threshold, not to the reception!"

He laughed, a true Dimitri laugh that she hadn't heard since before their breakup in Paris. "I can do both."

She wasn't about to spoil that smile, so she demurred.

He carried her all the way to the hotel ballroom where the reception was being held. A loud cheer went up when they came into the room and the next hour was spent accepting well wishes from their wedding guests.

Alexandra rested in one of the many Queen Anne style armchairs set in small groupings around the perimeter of the ballroom. Space had been left in the center of the floor for dancing. She was looking forward to being in Dimitri's arms.

"I guess he's not such a swine after all."

Alexandra smiled as her sister took the chair closest to her. "Hi, Maddy. Isn't this fabulous?" she asked, waving her hand to encompass the reception and its elegant guests. She was feeling incredibly happy for a woman who had just entered a marriage of convenience. It was all Dimitri's doing. "Can you believe the wedding?"

Madeleine grinned. "Believe it? I lived it. I was your matron of honor, after all. The horse drawn carriages were a very sweet touch. There were so many red and white poinsettias and that gorgeous Christmas greenery in the church, you couldn't see the pews."

"He did everything possible to make it special. He kept asking if there was anything else I wanted all week long, making sure my every fantasy of my wedding was fulfilled."

"And why should it not be?" Dimitri asked from behind her. He came to her side and rested his hand on the skin of her shoulder bared by the dropped shoulder neckline of her wedding dress. "You will only marry once. It should be the wedding of your dreams."

She tilted her head to smile up at him. "It has been."

He leaned down and kissed her softly on the lips. "I am glad, *yineka mou*. That was my only wish."

If she didn't know better, she'd say he sounded like a man in love. Even if he wasn't, he had to care about her a lot to have gone to so much trouble to see her happy.

"Making calf's eyes at each other again?" A man who could have been Dimitri's twin, but for his obvious younger age and dark brown eyes, slapped Dimitri on the back. "There will be plenty of time for that later."

Dimitri's hand on her shoulder tightened briefly in a reassuring gesture as if he could sense her unease.

"I do not make calf's eyes," he informed his brother.

Spiros smiled mockingly. "If you say so."

Phoebe, a beautiful woman with classic Greek features and an air of youthful innocence, laughed. "Do not tease your brother. A man is allowed to look pleased with his bride on his wedding day."

Remembering the picture she'd seen of Spiros and Phoebe's wedding day, Alexandra thought Phoebe must be intimately acquainted with the concept and said so.

Phoebe blushed sweetly while Spiros put his arm around her shoulder in a possessive manner. "This is true," he said.

Alexandra smiled. At least her pregnancy hadn't ruined their lives. They were obviously very happy to be married to each other. She couldn't help wondering what the Petronides family had been thinking to match a girl of Phoebe's gentle nature and obvious youth with an overwhelming man like Dimitri in the first place.

"It's not just reserved for the wedding day, you know. I'm still making calf's eyes at my wife," Hunter said as he joined the group, taking the chair closest to Madeleine.

Madeleine's air of complacent acceptance of such an accolade indicated whatever contretemps Alexandra's problems had caused in their marriage was well and truly over.

Alexandra looked up at Dimitri. She was not at all convinced he'd been looking at her with anything near the adoring glance her brother-in-law bestowed upon her sister. However, she was willing to tease him regardless. "So I can look forward to years of bovine expressions of affection?"

He stiffened with affront just as she'd expected him to do. "I am not a cow."

She smiled, feeling mischievous. "No indeed. If anything, you must be likened to a bull." She rubbed her protruding middle and felt their son move. "I would say that he is proof positive you are a male capable of breeding."

After a second of shocked silence, during which the entire group seemed to assimilate her rather risqué teasing, they all burst out laughing, including Dimitri. There were a few more teasing comments and Madeleine even went so far as to welcome Dimitri into the family which he thanked her for with grave appreciation rather than his usual arrogance.

After which, he leaned toward Alexandra and asked, "Are you ready to go?"

"We haven't danced yet." And she wanted to.

He smiled indulgently. "And we must do this to fulfill tradition, hmm?"

She nodded, loving the look of indulgence in his eyes. It made her feel cosseted.

He reached out his hand and led her to the middle of the ballroom floor, empty but for a few guests who stood in small groups chatting. Their presence on the dance floor was the orchestra's cue to move into a slow waltzing tune.

She and Dimitri took the traditional pose for a waltz, her train attached to her wrist making her feel like a nineteenth-century debutante at her comeout ball. Dimitri's dancing was divine and Alexandra lost herself in the pleasure of his arms and their bodies' movement to the music.

Other couples began to join them. Madeleine and Hunter. Phoebe and Spiros. Several guests she did not know by name.

She tilted her head to look into his eyes. "Thank you."

"For dancing with you?" he asked, a smile flirting with the edges of his lips.

"For all of this. The wedding. Keeping Mama calmed down over the last week. Charming Madeleine so she didn't think I was marrying an ogre. Buying the Dupree Mansion back for Mama. I guess I didn't think you were totally serious and yet you accomplished the purchase in less than a week. I'm stunned."

"I want you to be happy, *pethi mou*. I have told you this."

"Are all Petronides men willing to sacrifice for their wife's happiness?"

A shadow passed over his chiseled features, but was quickly gone. "All the Petronides males in my family, yes."

"That gives me a great deal of hope for the future, *mon cher*."

He stopped, stock-still in the middle of a turn.

"What's the matter?" she asked, anxiously. Had she stepped on his foot without realizing it?

"Say it again."

"What?" Then she knew. She hadn't called him by an endearment since he found her at Madeleine's. Even in the most passionate of their lovemaking, she had used only his name.

She could not deny him. He'd given her so much this week. She went up on tiptoes and still had to pull his head down so their lips could meet. *"Mon cher,"* she whispered against his lips before kissing him.

It was a kiss completely lacking in passion, a restoration of a bond that had been cruelly severed and left her bleeding. It had left its mark on Dimitri as well and now they saluted one another with a kiss of remembrance and renewal.

Three hours later, they were aboard Dimitri's private jet. She had changed into a comfortable, but chic honey gold, oversized, crocheted sweater and almond-colored wool stretch pants. Relaxed on the small couch in the plain's main cabin, she sipped on the glass of fruit juice Dimitri's personal flight attendant had given her.

"We should be taking off in less than half an hour," Dimitri informed her, walking into the main cabin from the cockpit after speaking to the pilot.

He had changed too and now wore tailored black slack trousers, a round-necked Armani sweater in gray over a black T-shirt. He lowered his long frame onto the sofa beside her, his outer thigh brushing her own sending the ever ready shivers down her limbs in anticipation of the next touch.

"How long will the flight to Athens take?" she asked, trying to tamp down the urge to slide her hands under his sweater and feel the well muscled contours of his chest.

He shrugged. "It depends. Perhaps eight hours."

"I'm glad I don't have to make the flight on a commercial airline. I don't think I could take it." So much sitting in one position would be painful to her back in her currently pregnant state.

His fingertips brushed her cheeks. "I would never expect you too." His hand fell away. "I did not ask if you were okay with changing doctors so late in your pregnancy."

"I can hardly have my New York doctor in Greece," she replied with a smile.

"So Madeleine said."

Her sister again. She bit back a grimace. "I'll be fine."

"I have arranged for you to be seen by an eminent obstetrician in Athens. He wants us to move to the Athens apartment for your last month."

"You've already spoken to him?" Why did that surprise her? This was his heir they were talking about after all.

"He comes highly recommended."

"I have no doubt," she said with some bemusement. So much for having to find a new doctor and arrange appointments for her last trimester.

"If you do not like him, we will find someone else."

Suddenly it struck her that Dimitri was worried about her reaction. She laid her hand over his. "I'll be fine. Really. Have you already arranged for my records to be transferred?"

"I had them faxed three days ago."

"Did I sign for that?" Between the marriage license, living Visa for Greece and other paperwork necessary for their wedding to take place, she didn't know what she had signed.

"Yes."

"Do you plan to be with me during delivery?"

"I would like this very much, but the final decision must be yours."

That surprised her. First that he wanted to be there. Dimitri wasn't exactly a New Man. And second that he would leave the choice to her. "I want you there."

"Then I will be. I believe there are classes we can take to help you through the delivery."

She stared at him, too shocked to speak this time.

"What is the matter? Do you not wish to take these classes? I had heard they were very beneficial for new mothers. I think you should consider attending them."

"I had always planned to do so," she choked out.

"You do not wish me to attend with you? Someone must be your coach. As your husband, I should fulfill the role." He was arguing with her like she'd denied him.

She hadn't. Didn't he realize how much she had wanted to share her pregnancy with the father of her baby? She'd dreamed of taking childbirth classes with Dimitri, but had known her fantasies were unattainable. Cold reality had been a life without him and the prospect of giving birth alone.

"I want you to be my labor coach. I want that more than anything." Then she burst into tears.

Dimitri looked like he'd just been hit by a truck. It would be funny, if she wasn't feeling so emotional.

"Alexandra, *yineka mou,* what is it?"

She shook her head and tried to stem the flow of tears, but the salty wetness kept up a steady flow down her cheeks.

"You must not upset yourself this way."

"I'm n-not upset," she sobbed.

"Come here." He took her glass from her hand and set it down, then pulled her into his arms and onto his lap. Just like in the limo. "Tell me what is making you cry." He sounded quite desperate.

"I wanted you to be there so many times. I would wake up and reach for you and only find an empty bed. The first time the baby really kicked, I wanted to call you, but I thought you were married. I m-missed you so much…"

His arms tightened around her and he whispered to her in Greek. The words were too low and quick for her to understand, but the soothing tone was not. She snuggled into his arms and cried out the frustration and pain of the last three months.

Her sobs eventually turned to small hiccups and he mopped up her face as if she were a child. She gave him a watery smile. "You'll be good with the baby."

He didn't respond to the joke. His eyes had darkened with unfathomable emotion. "You will never be without me again."

As vows went, that was a pretty comforting one. She nodded, accepting his words and the promise in his eyes.

CHAPTER TEN

HER tears were killing him. And she'd cried like this for a solid month after leaving Paris? The thought sent shards of pain slicing through him.

This was his woman. His wife. He had almost lost her. He would never let her go again. She had wanted him and he hadn't been there. He didn't want her to cry anymore. He wanted to look toward the future, for her to see things were going to be different.

He knew the truth now, who and what she was beyond the fashion model with an almost obsessive focus on her career. He understood that focus now. She'd been supporting her family, her mother now, but presumably Madeleine also until she had married Hunter. Alexandra hadn't been able to give up her career to travel with him because she had needed the money and she'd not wanted to take it from him.

His arms tightened around her of their own accord. She filled his arms so perfectly, their baby nestled between their bodies. Her tears were lessening, but had not stopped. He knew of only one way to completely overcome her outburst of emotion.

It was with the one thing he had not managed to kill between them with his actions three months ago. Passion.

Possessive pleasure coursed through him as he turned her face upward until he could cover her tear-drenched lips with his own. She belonged to him now, both legally and with the emotional ties of carrying his child. He did not have to seduce her into accepting his kisses. She tasted so sweet and her response was even sweeter. Her mouth opened under his on a small gasp and he deepened the kiss with one thought in mind.

He wanted to obliterate her sadness and replace it with pleasure in his arms.

He plundered her mouth, his own desire soon surging through him in unstoppable waves. She responded with all the generous eroticism that was in her nature, her hands coming up to cling to his shoulders, her mouth moving under his with enticing need. He wanted her under him, surrounding his sex, yielding her softness to the hardness that made him a man.

He needed to touch her. His hands were working their way under the hem of her sweater when a sound from the anterior of the cabin reminded him where they were. On his plane. Readying for takeoff. The flight attendant would be requesting them to buckle-up any moment now. The woman had probably already gotten an eyeful. He forced himself to pull back and gently set Alexandra from him.

She didn't understand at first and almost overcame his self-control trying to get back in his arms, but all at once she also seemed to realize what they were doing and where they were. Eyes gold with desire went round and wide while the pale perfection of her skin turned a rosy hue from embarrassment.

She primly straightened her sweater over the pants that clung to her sexy legs. "I forgot where we were."

He smiled. "I also."

She shot a sideways glance at the flight attendant who was pretending to be very busy in the galley.

"She's as discomforted as you are," he assured Alexandra.

"Is that meant to make me feel better like telling me a spider is more frightened of me than I am of it?" she asked, her blushing cheeks now almost fire engine red.

Unable to help himself, he reached out and cupped her nape. He needed to touch her in some way. "They are both the truth."

She cast another glance at the flight attendant, whose back was to them while she moved things around the galley in an obvious attempt to give them privacy. "I'm willing to buy the embarrassment thing, but not the spider theory."

He rubbed the delicate skin of her neck with his thumb. "After we have reached altitude, we can retire to the relative privacy of the bedroom."

That brought a smile, a very feminine, flirtatious smile. "You mean so I can get my sleep? Pregnant ladies need lots of rest, or so some domineering father-to-be has been telling me all week long."

He smiled at her reminder that she had not always taken his concern for her welfare with good grace. "I will assure you get your rest."

"Before or after?" she asked, her eyes sparkling with teasing lights he'd thought never to see again.

It *was* going to be all right. He would make it so. "After, most definitely after."

She gave an exaggerated sigh and clasped her hands, fluttering her eyelashes like a 1920's film star. "I can't wait."

The minx. "I'll make it worth your while," he promised, knowing that in this, he could satisfy her every desire.

"I'll see that you do."

Alexandra stood before Dimitri, divested of her travel clothes, her body throbbing with a desire he had fed until she was ready to scream for fulfillment. And that was before he undressed her. He was equally naked and his body's desire was apparent in the glorious size and rigidity of his erection.

His eyes were intent, appearing almost black in the dimmed lighting of the plane's bedroom. "You are so beautiful."

She felt the words clear to her toes and other nether regions that affected her breathing and her ability to stand. "I feel beautiful when you look at me like that, not like a misshapen woman with a football for a waistline."

"Misshapen?" His expression turned feral. "You are carrying my child. Your shape is the biggest turn-on imaginable. I get hard every time you turn sideways and I get a picture of the difference my son has made in your body."

She turned in silhouette, purposefully, provocatively and invitingly.

He accepted the invitation with all the speed of a jaguar going in for the kill. As prepared as she thought she was, she still squealed in the most embarrassing way when he swept her into his arms and then onto the bed in one heady rush.

He rolled onto his back and pulled her on top of him, spreading her legs so she was poised above his manhood, kissing him intimately. "You control how deep," was all he said.

And she did, sliding onto him centimeter by tantalizing centimeter. The feel of his hardness filling her so completely was incredible. She couldn't take all of him comfortably any longer, but he didn't push her or complain. He didn't seem disappointed at all if the look of intense ecstasy on his face was any indication.

While he allowed her to dictate the level of his penetration, he set the pace by holding her hips in an unshakable grip and moving her slowly and gently on his shaft. Her eyes slid shut as sensation crowded through her. How could she have survived months without this?

The answer was: she hadn't. She had spent that time living as half a person, hating him, missing him and wishing with all her heart things were different.

But now she was once again connected to the other half of herself and she celebrated the bliss that connection gave her. She forced her eyes open again. She wanted to see him, see the effect of their joining on *him*.

His eyes were slits, his face rock hard with passionate need. His grip on her hips was almost bruising, but she didn't complain. She needed to know she could push him to this place of no control. It gave her hope that his feelings for her were something more than guilt and responsibility, or even run-of-the-mill desire. There was nothing ordinary about the feelings they sparked in each other.

He increased the pace of their loving and she gasped as the pleasure increased as her insides began to tighten toward that ultimate satisfaction only he had ever given her. She couldn't support herself anymore and she whimpered, knowing she could not just collapse on top of him.

He seemed to understand her need because he rolled them both to the side, keeping their bodies intimately connected, pulling her thigh over his own. He took over the thrusting, holding her to him with a hand cupped possessively on her backside. Now that her hands were no longer occupied with holding her up, she could touch him. She brushed her fingers through the black silk of his chest hair and he shuddered.

She smiled, remembering what made him shudder even more and began to run light circles around his male nipples. When they were hard, she pinched them and his body bowed toward her in animalistic joy. She cried out as his body brushed hers in abandoned desire. The inner contractions started and she lost sense of time and place as her body convulsed in wave after wave of ecstatic delight.

His release was accompanied by a feral shout that left her eardrums ringing. The ecstasy of their union went on and on until they lay spent and sweating. He brushed his hand down her shoulder and her entire body contracted on another wave of pleasure. She moaned. It was too much.

He pulled her closer, until she was resting against him, shivering with intermittent aftershocks from their cataclysmic release. He soothed her with a hand on her back. "Shh. It's all right."

A sob welled up in her. "It's too much."

The calming motion of his hand did not stop. "No, *agapi mou,* it is so wonderful your body can barely stand it, but it is not too much."

Everything in her went still. Had he called her his love? Then reason asserted itself. After something as incredible as what they had just shared, any man would be forgiven for using such a tender term with his partner. It was just sex talk, but even so, it made her feel good and she hugged the endearment close to her heart.

She sighed and snuggled closer. "Relative privacy is right. If your crew didn't hear you shouting, they're deaf."

"I was not the only one making noise, hmm?"

She smiled against his chest. "I'm not answering."

Masculine laughter rumbled in his chest, vibrating through her. "I do not need this answer. I have ears to hear."

She didn't reply and they rested together in silence for several minutes before he shifted away from her. She murmured a protest, but he picked her up and carried her into the plane's small shower, where he proceeded to wash her so thoroughly she made a lot more noise and could not stand unaided when he was finished. He carried her back to bed and she fell asleep as he pulled her body snugly into his own.

She didn't know how long she slept, but when she woke, the lighting was no longer dimmed and Dimitri lay beside her watching her with an intent expression she could not decipher.

She smiled at him. "Hi. You're watching me."

"You are beautiful when you sleep."

Her smile turned wry. "Right. I bet my hair is sticking on end and I'm not wearing a speck of makeup."

A gentle finger traced the contours of her face. "You do not need makeup and your hair is very sexy."

She scooted into a sitting position. "I'm hungry."

He swung out of bed. "Stay where you are. I will order some food."

He pulled on a robe hanging in the miniscule closet and went into the main cabin. Which just went to show the difference between them. While she had modeled lingerie on the catwalks of Paris, she couldn't have faced the flight attendant in her bathrobe to save her life.

Dimitri was back fifteen minutes later carrying a tray laden with food. He laid it across her lap, dropped his robe and slid back into bed beside her. She ate a bowl of wild rice and mushroom soup, a crusty roll, and a brownie before sitting back against him, replete.

He pulled away from her long enough to set the tray on the floor. Settling back into their previous position, he laid his hand on the baby. Their son kicked and rolled, making both of them laugh. "He's very active in there, my son. He will be champion football player, that one."

"More like he'll keep us running with his antics."

"If he is anything like his mother, he will keep me on my toes until my hair turns gray."

She smiled at that and laid her hand over Dimitri's. "You know, you never did explain how you came to the conclusion the baby is yours."

"I told you about my friend."

"The doctor? Yes. I remember. That explains how, but not why. I mean just because you realized it was possible for you to be the father of my child, didn't mean you had to believe you were the father."

Dimitri exhaled a long breath. "I knew the truth long before I went to Nikos and asked him how it could be possible."

"Why?"

She felt his body go tense against her and she lifted her head off his chest to look into his eyes. They weren't revealing anything. "My mother and father died in an avalanche when I was ten years old."

"I know." It was the only thing he'd told her about his parents and one of the few things she knew about his family.

"My father was bringing her back from the ski lodge where she had been staying with her current lover."

"Current lover?"

Dimitri nodded, his head moving in a precise movement that was painful to watch. "She fell in love with daunting regularity, only one of those times was with my father."

She laid her hand over his heart and caressed the skin there in a comforting gesture. "Oh, Dimitri…"

He frowned as if her sympathy bothered him. It probably did. He was a very proud man.

"She had left before. There was even some question as to whether or not Spiros could claim the Petronides bloodline. My father insisted on having the tests done, my grandfather told me, not because he didn't love my brother but because he wanted to squelch the rumors. I believe he would have paid to have the tests doctored if they had come back negative. They did not."

"But if your mother was unfaithful, why did your father remain married to her?" She could not imagine a proud Petronides male doing so.

Dimitri's frown turned to a scowl. "He was obsessed with her. He too called this feeling love. Their marriage was volatile, their reunions dramatic but in the end her concept of love and his obsession killed them both."

No wonder Dimitri had such a jaundiced view of love. A depressing sense of hopelessness came over her. Would he ever allow himself that level of vulnerability after the example his parents had set him?

"It is not a pretty tale."

But it explained why he hadn't trusted her. He'd seen too much at an impressionable young age to take the fidelity of a woman for granted.

"We all have memories we would rather forget. Every family has its skeletons."

"Not according to your mother."

Alexandra smiled at his attempt at humor, but it was a small one. She didn't feel like laughing when she'd come face to face with Dimitri's reason for distrusting love. "Not all women are like your mother."

He shrugged. "Adultery is not such an uncommon thing."

"Is that why you were so sure I'd had a lover?"

He'd been waiting for her to betray him like his mother had done, because her betrayal had not only been against her husband. She'd done terrible emotional damage to her children as well.

The tension in him grew almost palpable. "It shames me, but yes."

"My unexplained trips must have played upon your fears."

"I was not afraid."

Right. "You don't like discussing your feelings, do you?" Why hadn't she caught on to that before?

"No, but you asked for a reason for my belief."

"Your mother's behavior explains why you didn't trust me. It does not explain what changed your mind."

"I realized you were not like her."

Hope erupted in her like Mount Vesuvius. If he already accepted she was nothing like his mother, he might eventually learn to trust her enough to let himself love her.

"I'm not," she reiterated for good measure. Then, because she was curious and couldn't help wanting to know, she asked, "When did you realize it?"

"When I returned to the apartment and found the pregnancy test on top of the lingerie."

"Oh." So, those final frantic moments in the apartment hadn't been wasted.

"There was a message in that, was there not?"

"Yes."

"You connected the pregnancy with our lovemaking."

He really did understand how her mind worked. "Did it make you remember what it had been like between us?" That was what she had intended.

"Yes." His expression was grim. "I knew you could not be that way with someone else. I still did not understand why you took trips you refused to explain to me, but I knew they were not to meet another man."

"Now you know."

"Now I know." His expression lightened and the hand on her shoulder ventured lower. "I know something else as well."

"Oh, what's that?" she asked breathlessly. That hand had found an already aching peak and gently tweaked it.

"There are things I would rather do with you than talk."

"I'm so surprised." She tried to sound mocking, but his touch was affecting her and her voice came out husky instead.

They spent a week in Athens, Dimitri insisting they have a honeymoon before he took her to the family home to meet his grandfather. It was a blissful seven days filled with touristy stuff and making love, lots and lots of making love.

Dimitri took her to see the obstetrician. She turned bright red and wanted to hide in a closet when Dimitri insisted on verifying her former obstetrician's advice about making love. He wasn't content until the doctor had done a full examination and Dimitri even requested an ultrasound to check the progress of the baby.

At four months, she hadn't been able to make out much on the ultrasound, but this time she didn't need the doctor to tell her where the baby's head and feet were. Nor did she need his interpretation to affirm the male sex of her child.

She pointed to the baby sucking its thumb in the womb and turned to share her delight with Dimitri. He was pale and his eyes had the dazed look of someone in serious shock.

"Mr. Petronides, are you all right?" the doctor asked.

"Dimitri?" she prompted when he didn't answer.

He turned to her, his eyes suspiciously bright. "That is my son. You nurture and protect him with your body. How can I ever thank you for this gift?"

She stared at him, nonplussed. She knew fatherhood had affected him strongly, but this was over the top…and she loved it. "No thanks necessary. He is my gift as well, *mon cher*."

Then Dimitri bent down and kissed her lips very gently as she lay on the examining table with the ultrasound gel making her tummy glisten.

The doctor looked on with tolerance. "You will be an indulgent papa I fear," he said.

Dimitri straightened to his full six foot, four inches and smiled. "Perhaps."

And Alexandra felt suffused with a glow of contentment.

That contentment lasted until Dimitri told her it was time for her to meet his grandfather.

"But what if he hates me?" she asked nervously. "He has every reason."

"Don't worry. He cannot help but adore you and he has no reason to hate you."

She would probably have been more confident of that concept if she were confident in Dimitri's adoration. But while he was overtly affectionate, complimentary and the charming companion she remembered, he never spoke words of love. He'd never called her his love again either. Not in Greek, not in English or even French which they slipped into frequently, it being the language they had originally used to communicate.

Love words never passed his lips…even in the height of passion.

CHAPTER ELEVEN

THEOPOLIS PETRONIDES did not look at all like a seventy-one-year-old man who had undergone heart by-pass surgery only a few months ago. Even leaning on a cane for support, he stood commandingly tall in the middle of the spacious Mediterranean-style room. His almost black eyes bore into Alexandra with disconcerting force from below steel-gray brows that matched the hair on his head.

"So this is my new granddaughter, heh?" He put his hand out commandingly. "Come here and greet your family, child."

Alexandra stepped forward with an assumed air of confidence, knowing to show her fear of his disapproval would be to lose his respect. She put her hands on his shoulders and reached up to kiss his cheek in greeting. He returned the salute with an approving smile before she stepped back.

"She doesn't look like her pictures," he said to Dimitri. Then he turned back to Alexandra. "I like you better this way. More natural. No fancy curls and dye jobs in your hair. My Sophia, she never used color on her hair." His gaze roamed over her face like he was taking inventory. "Eyes a nice hazel, not some impossible green. It suits you."

She bit back a smile at his blunt speaking. "Thank you. Dimitri thought maybe I was too ugly to support myself modeling any longer."

Both men spoke at once.

"I did not say—"

"What's the matter with my grandson?"

The smile broke through. "To be fair, I did look a fright from lack of sleep and morning sickness at the time."

Mr. Petronides beetled his brows at Dimitri. "Never tell a pregnant woman she looks a fright, even when her appearance would be enough to scare the goats from the hills. You will find yourself sleeping in the guest room and dealing with enough tears to sink a fishing boat, heh?"

"A little piece of wisdom Grandmother taught you?" Dimitri asked.

"My eyes. She taught me." He thumped his cane on the floor. "She asked me did I think she was fat? Of course she was fat. She was as round as a barrel and could barely walk. Your papa, he weighed ten pounds. She almost died. I said no more babies after that, I can tell you." Remembered fear clouded the old man's eyes for a moment. "I told her, yes I thought she'd gotten fat. She threw her dinner at me and then started in on the other dishes on the table. I said I was sorry and ended up with moussaka in my hair for my trouble. I ran for my life."

Dimitri's smile made Alexandra feel all gooey inside while she laughed at Mr. Petronides's story. "And she made you sleep in the guest room?"

He grinned and winked. "She locked our door."

"So you meekly found another bed for the night, hmm?" Dimitri asked mockingly.

Mr. Petronides laughed. "You are like me. Tell me what you would do if this lovely creature carrying my first great-grandson locked you out of her room." He waved his cane in Alexandra's direction.

Remembering a locked door and a very erotic shower, she smiled. No wonder Mr. Petronides had his security man teach Dimitri to pick a lock. For some reason that thought struck her as terribly funny and she started laughing so hard she was almost bent over double.

"So it's already happened, heh?"

Dimitri didn't answer, but took her firmly by the wrist and pulled her to a bright red armchair and almost pushed her into it. "The baby can't be getting enough oxygen with you laughing like a loon," he reproved her, but his eyes smiled and the corner of his mouth was engagingly tilted.

She took a deep breath and then another, finally managing to stop her mirth.

Mr. Petronides sat across from her, his face creased in a smile. "I did not have a smart grandfather to see to my education. I did not know how to pick a lock, so I threatened to kick in the door. She started crying so loud I could hear her through the thick wood." He rolled his eyes. "I climbed in through the window and took her by surprise, heh? It was a very satisfactory reunion."

Alexandra felt herself blush thinking of Dimitri's similar approach to the same problem.

He sat on the arm of her chair with his hand on her nape. "Are Spiros and Phoebe back in Paris?" he asked his grandfather.

"Yes. They came here first, though. Wanted to tell me what a wonderful new granddaughter I had."

Alexandra felt her cheeks heating again. She smiled at the older man. "I'm pleased they think so. I was worried they would resent me, but they were very kind as you have been."

Mr. Petronides waved his hand in an expansive Greek gesture. "It all worked out for the best, heh? I have both my grandsons married, a grandchild on the way and everyone is happy as a clam. Sophia could not have done a better job if she were alive to arrange it all," he said with obvious satisfaction. "I think I must send prayers of thanks to the Good God above for so many gifts all at once to my family."

His clear sincerity moved her deeply. She impulsively pushed herself out of the chair and crossed to give him another kiss on the cheek. "Thank you. You are a very nice man."

He waved her away, but his eyes revealed his pleasure in her words. "Take her upstairs, Dimitrius. Pregnant ladies need their rest, heh?"

Which made her giggle again, being so close to what Dimitri said at least once a day since his return into her life. They were usually followed by his version of a nap, the resemblance to which was loosely based on the fact they went to bed.

Dimitri shook his head and swung her up against his chest. "Come, *pethi mou.* I believe you need an afternoon nap."

She went off into gales of laughter at that, but she choked back her amusement to protest. "You can't carry me up the stairs. I'm too heavy."

Dimitri's eyes glittered down at her. "I won't be accused of implying you're fat. I learned my lesson from Grandfather's story."

"Letting me walk on my own isn't making any sort of implication," she asserted.

He was already a third of the way up the stairs. "It is after you said you were too heavy. Either you're implying you are fat or I am a wimp. I refuse to give credence to either."

She subsided, secretly thrilled at his macho display of consideration.

He carried her into a bedroom so big that even the extra-long, king-size four-poster bed looked small in the middle of it. Two sets of side-by-side sliding glass doors looked out onto the wrap around terrace and the crystalline-blue sea beyond it and her gaze alighted there first.

"It's breathtaking, *mon cher*."

He let her slide down his body in a very suggestive manner and she turned from the incredible view to smile into his blue eyes. "A *nap* I think you said?"

"We must make sure you are properly tired," he informed her as he began working on the removal of her clothes.

Her gaze wandered around the room and was arrested by a familiar Lladro figurine on top of an antique chest of drawers. It was of a young girl in a garden. Dimitri had said the figure reminded him of Alexandra. The last time she'd seen it, it had been in a pile of paper wrapping on the floor of the living room in the Paris apartment.

She only had time to ponder the significance of it being here in Greece for a few moments before Dimitri's expert ministrations shut down her thinking processes entirely.

Alexandra pulled open yet another drawer in the antique bureau looking for her clothes. So far she had found a drawer full of Dimitri's socks, one full of silk boxers, another had the plain cotton t-shirts he liked to wear under sweaters or by themselves with jeans when he was relaxing at home. She closed the drawer and bent down to open the last one.

She'd opened it only a couple of inches when strong hands on her arms pulled her into a standing position. "*Pethi mou,* what are you doing? You should not be bending over like that and opening heavy drawers."

"I'm just looking for my clothes, but so far all I've found are yours." She looked in disgust at the last open drawer. Dimitri's stuff again.

A small piece of white caught her eye and she found herself kneeling again to see what it was. She reached in and pulled the plastic stick from the drawer. She stared at it in her hand. *He'd saved the pregnancy test.*

Turning her head so she could see his face, she asked, "Why did you save it?"

"It was the only proof I had that my baby existed. I could not find you. I did not know where to look, but somewhere my baby was growing in your womb." Red scorched the chiseled lines of his cheekbones. "It gave me hope."

She felt emotion well up in her and she shot to her feet, probably too fast for a woman almost six months pregnant, but she didn't care. She threw her arms around him and hugged him tightly to her. "Oh, Dimitri…"

His arms closed around her toweling robe-clad figure and she felt a sense of belonging she had not felt since before she left Paris.

"So, where are my clothes?" she asked into his naked chest.

He let her go and turned her toward a doorway in the wall beside the entrance to the en suite bathroom. "There."

She went over and opened the door to find a large dressing room with three walls of hanging clothes and one of built in shelves, drawers and shoe racks. The sight of Dimitri's suits hanging beside her pregnancy dresses had an air of domesticity that made her smile. She reached for one of the dresses to wear for dinner with his grandfather when she realized several of the garments were from the pile she'd left in Paris.

"You saved my clothes," she said stupidly.

"Of course. I knew you would be returning and in need of them," he said from the open doorway. "Though not for a few months. I should have bought you more maternity things. I did not think."

She fingered the brilliant blue of an ankle length silk sheath dress Dimitri had bought her in Milan. Had he kept her clothes for a similar reason to keeping the pregnancy test?

She turned and gave him a saucy smile. "Are you saying I'm fat?"

His eyes filled with mock horror. "God forbid. I would not say such a thing. Your figure is luscious and perfect."

Right at that moment she was so happy it felt like champagne bubbles fizzing in her bloodstream. "You're a pretty fine specimen yourself, Mr. Petronides."

He would be afraid to admit he loved her after the experience he'd had growing up. But she was beginning to believe in the impossible...that he could love her and need her in her own right, not just as the mother of his child.

"If I stay in here, we will not make it to dinner with my grandfather."

She shooed him out. "Then go. I have to get dressed."

She pulled on a pair of peach silk bikini briefs and matching bra she'd bought since getting pregnant. Over that she slid on an apricot sundress with a flirty skirt. The soft fabric fell in graceful curves over her tummy to midcalf. She loved the dress because it made her feel feminine even though she'd lost her waistline weeks ago.

She walked out of the dressing room to find Dimitri ready to go down in a dinner suit, silk shirt and understated tie.

Approval burned in his eyes when he looked at her. "I'm tempted to order dinner in our room tonight."

She gave him a severe look. "Don't you dare. I want to make a good impression on your grandfather."

"You already have, or couldn't you tell?"

"He's terribly nice."

Dimitri's dark brows rose. "When he wants to be."

"Well, I'm glad he wants to be nice to me."

"You are family."

She smiled, feeling warm inside. To be accepted simply because she was family and not because she did and said all the right things was a unique experience for her. She liked it.

Halfway through dinner, Dimitri was called from the table to take an international phone call.

Mr. Petronides winked at her. "Ah, the business, it intrudes, eh?"

She lifted her shoulders in a small, casual movement. "He must have a lot of catching up to do after all his time in New York and on our honeymoon."

"As you say." He beetled his brows at her in what was becoming a familiar gesture. "Tell me about your family."

So she did, telling him about Madeleine and Hunter, her mother and Dimitri's generosity in buying back the Dupree Mansion.

Mr. Petronides flicked his hand in a throw away gesture. "This is nothing to Dimitrius. Your mother is now his family. It is his responsibility to look after her."

Alexandra chewed her lip anxiously. "I did not marry your grandson so he would take over my financial responsibilities with my mother."

The old man laughed, long and richly. "Of course not, silly child. Had you wanted money from my grandson, you would never have left Paris."

She smiled with relief. "You're right. All I ever wanted was him. I didn't know about Phoebe," she added earnestly.

"*Ne.* Yes. I know."

"I'm sorry."

"For what are you sorry child?"

"Causing Dimitri to break his promise to you."

Mr. Petronides nodded his head knowingly. "You feel the weight of such things. I like this."

"Thank you." She wasn't all that fond of the guilt that plagued her, though.

"But I do not want you to feel badly my grandson could not keep a promise he made under the threat of my health." He sighed. "I should not have put such a pressure on him."

"He told me in Paris that his marriage to Phoebe had been expected for a long time," she said with a small spark of residual pain. She frowned. "You must have been very disappointed."

"*Disappointed?*" He looked startled, his dark eyes wide for a second of stunned silence. "I wanted the certainty of great-grandchildren and I have that now, heh?" he asked with a pointed look at her stomach, not quite hidden by the table.

She felt herself blushing…again. The Petronides men were not good for her composure.

He laughed again, this time with wholly masculine amusement. "Do not worry about Dimitrius breaking his promise to marry Phoebe. It all worked out for the best, heh? Phoebe is happier with Spiros, I think. She's a little afraid of Dimitri. I did not see this until after the betrothal was announced and they were here together."

It astounded her, but no one in Dimitri's family seemed bitter with her over the changes her pregnancy had wrought among them.

He took a sip of his wine. "And this grandson of mine, he kept his second promise, heh?"

"Second promise?"

"He married you just as he promised me he would." Dark eyes glittered with steely determination. "He gave my great-grandson the Petronides name. *Ne*, yes, I am a content man."

Shock congealed the smile on Alexandra's face. "He promised you he would marry me?"

Mr. Petronides nodded his gray head. "He is a man of his word, my grandson. His second promise more than negated his first," he said with pride. "Your son will be raised a Petronides. I could die tomorrow happy."

"Don't talk like that," she admonished even as her heart was breaking within her.

Dimitri had *promised* his grandfather he would marry her? He had *promised* to give their son the Petronides name?

"The young. They fear talk of death. I am old. I do not fear it, but I would like to teach my great-grandson to pick a lock before I go." He laughed at his own joke.

She forced her lips to smile. "I thought it was your security man who taught Dimitri?"

"He did, but I made him teach me too so I could

teach Spiros. Maybe Phoebe has a surprise to come one day, heh?''

Alexandra couldn't believe she could carry on a conversation with Dimitri's grandfather and pretend nothing was wrong while inside she felt like she was dying.

Dimitri had not married her because he wanted *her*. He hadn't even married her for the baby's sake. *He'd married her because he had made a promise to his grandfather.* His brother had prevented him from keeping the first promise, a huge blow to his Greek pride. However nothing, not even her angry rejection had been able to stop him from keeping the second one.

No wonder Dimitri had put up with so much from her. He had been determined to keep his oath to his grandfather, no matter what obstacles she put in his path. When she had refused to discuss the option of marriage, he had seduced her. He had charmed her mother and even used the repurchase of Dupree Mansion as an incentive to get her to marry him.

In the back of her mind, she'd thought all that effort must mean he cared, that he would have given up and accepted visitation if she didn't matter to him personally. Now she knew differently. He might not love her, but he loved his grandfather…enough to marry the mistress that hadn't been proper marriage material before.

How could she have forgotten that? Dimitri had dismissed the idea of a future with her out of hand. And gullible idiot that she was, she'd conveniently ignored that fact when he started talking marriage. For the first time since agreeing to marry Dimitri, she felt bile rise in the back of her throat.

She took a hasty sip of her fruit juice and prayed the nausea would go away.

''Are you all right, child? You look pale.''

She looked down at her half-eaten dinner. "Just tired and maybe a little sick," she admitted. "Morning sickness did not go away after the first trimester like it's supposed to." But it had for a while.

Mr. Petronides nodded knowingly. "I remember. Do you want to lie down?"

Did she? She could hide from her misery upstairs, or end up wallowing in it. She really didn't want her own company right now. "I'd rather stay here with you."

"Ah, kindness to an old man."

"Not at all. I enjoy your company," she replied truthfully.

"Then tell me about this job you had. I have never met a fashion model."

She told him about her life as Xandra Fortune and ended up talking about how she had met Dimitri. Impossibly, she found herself laughing over memories of her life with Dimitri before she'd gotten pregnant.

She and Mr. Petronides had gone to the drawing room for coffee when Dimitri rejoined them. She was telling his grandfather about the first argument they'd ever had.

"I was doing a swimsuit cover. Dimitri came to the shoot on a whim."

"I came back a day early and surprised her," Dimitri inserted as he walked into the room.

Her head snapped around and she met his eyes briefly before her own gaze skated away. She didn't know how she managed it, but she didn't stand up and harangue him like a fishwife for once again withholding a crucial piece of information from her. For letting her believe he might be coming to love her when he'd been motivated by his personal sense of honor, not personal need.

Dimitri joined her on the brightly colored Mediterranean-style sofa. Her body tensed in response to his nearness. If only she could forget what he made her feel as easily as he conveniently forgot to tell her about his second promise.

She focused her attention on Mr. Petronides who was smiling benevolently at them. "He didn't like the suit I was wearing for the shoot and demanded I go to the trailer and take it off."

"So, being a reasonable woman and understanding the possessiveness of a traditional Greek male, you immediately changed, heh?" Mr. Petronides's eyes twinkled mockingly.

Dimitri snorted. "She threatened to take it off right there in front of everyone if I didn't shut up and go to the sidelines." He still sounded chagrined by her tactics.

She allowed herself a brief glance at him, but it hurt too much to make full frontal contact so she looked back at his grandfather. "It worked."

The older man roared with laughter and said something rapid to Dimitri in Greek that she didn't catch. Dimitri scowled.

She smiled. Anything that made him frown made her happy, or so she told herself.

"She has led you a merry chase, has she not, Dimitrius?"

Dimitri laid his arm across her shoulders. "Yes, but I have her now and I'm not letting go."

She wanted to cuddle into his side and kick him in the shin at the same time. Was she going crazy? She must be. And he was the one driving her there.

She jumped up. "I think I'll go to bed." She turned to Dimitri. "You needn't feel obligated to join me. I'm sure you and your grandfather have a great deal to catch up on." The words were stilted, but they were the best she could do.

Dimitri's eyes narrowed and he stood. "I will see you upstairs."

His grandfather stood as well, slowly coming to his feet, the expression on his face one of fatigue. It was the first time since she'd met him that he had shown a glimmer of the effects of his recent ill health. "Do not return downstairs for my sake, Dimitrius. Both the very old and the very young need their rest. I will find my bed."

She gave the old man a quick kiss on the cheek before turning to go upstairs.

Dimitri stayed behind a few moments saying goodnight to his grandfather, but caught up with her before she had reached the top of the stairs. She allowed him to take her hand, but when he reached for her later in bed she told him she was too tired to make love.

He'd married her because of a promise to a sick relative. For the first time she felt an unwelcome weight around her heart because of her pregnancy. If she hadn't gotten pregnant, Dimitri would have let her go without a second thought.

Even if Phoebe had still ended up married to Spiros, Dimitri wouldn't have gone looking for his discarded lover, Xandra Fortune.

Because his grandfather would not have extracted that second promise.

CHAPTER TWELVE

THE next morning Alexandra came to consciousness alone in the bed. She cuddled Dimitri's pillow, inhaling his scent, wishing his absence from their bed was not a physical ache in her heart. He had left for Athens two hours ago, but not before waking Alexandra with slow, tender caresses that had ended in such exquisite release she'd cried.

She'd gone to sleep determined not to make love with him. That determination hadn't lasted past his first drugging kiss around dawn. She rolled onto her back and stared at the ceiling. There were no answers to her predicament in the white plaster.

A knock on the door heralded the arrival of a maid with the breakfast Dimitri had ordered for her. She scooted into a sitting position and allowed the maid to lay the breakfast tray over her legs. An unexpected smile tilted her lips when she saw the dry toast, fruit, eggs and single slice of bacon. He'd teased her about her tendency to order the same meal for breakfast every morning. He'd said pregnant women were supposed to crave pickles and ice cream, not dry toast and bacon.

The food was accompanied by the awful tasting herbal tea she'd taken to drinking in the morning to settle her nausea. She ignored it, grateful the stomach upset that had plagued her the night before was gone. She refused to contemplate the possibility Dimitri's lovemaking had been more effective in making her feel better than all the herbal tea she'd drunk.

The maid opened the curtains letting in the bright Greek sun before leaving Alexandra to finish her breakfast alone.

She ate by rote, her thoughts casting back to the night before and then more recently to earlier that morning. She still tingled in places from her husband's possession. Remembered pleasure caused an unwelcome throbbing in her lower body. If he were here now, she'd be hard pressed not to beg him to make love to her.

Huffing out a sigh of frustration at her body's betrayal, she climbed out of bed. As she showered and dressed, she considered her situation pragmatically. What, after all, had changed? She'd known Dimitri didn't love her when she agreed to marry him.

But she hadn't known about the promise, her heart cried.

Did it matter?

Of course it mattered. It was humiliating to realize she'd been married for a reason totally unrelated to herself. She had her pride.

And it had been a cold companion for three long months in New York. She'd been miserable without him. She'd missed him like a wound in her soul every day they had been apart, even believing he had been married to another woman hadn't dulled the unwanted desire to be back in his arms.

She walked over to the dresser and picked up the Lladro statue. It was so delicate. She could remember with absolute clarity her sense of joy and wonder when he had bought it for her. She ran her forefinger along the figurine's head and the graceful lines of her dress. Then she lightly touched the kitten playing at the woman's feet.

Dimitri had saved this reminder of a happier time between them. He had saved her clothes. He had brought her things here, to the family home, obviously believing she would live here as well one day. Of course he had believed it. He knew about his promise to his grandfather, her mind insidiously reminded her.

But he hadn't had to save her things. She'd left them in an insulting pile on the floor, flouting his pride, condemning him with their presence and her absence.

She had a choice. She could fight the truth and make both Dimitri and herself miserable, or she could accept reality.

She and Dimitri would have the kind of marriage people in his world and her mother's world excelled at...a marriage of convenience. After all, she was no longer Xandra Fortune, the nobody model he slept with, but Alexandra Petronides, his wife and a woman with a background he could be proud of.

Sharp slashes of pain cut at her heart at the last thought. She'd spent her whole life being accepted for the trappings of who she was. Her own mother had withheld her love and approval for the six long years Alexandra had spent as Xandra Fortune. Cecelia had been effusive in her approval the week before the wedding though. She had been thrilled her daughter had landed such a catch in the marriage market.

And she'd positively gushed her appreciation for her oldest daughter when Dimitri repurchased the Dupree Mansion.

Alexandra thought of the empty years ahead being nothing more than the traditional Greek wife, an adjunct in Dimitri's life, not a major player. She determined then and there not to fall passively into that role. She'd married Dimitri as she'd said she would. Their son would be raised a Petronides.

Because she loved Dimitri, she would never leave him. But she wasn't going to play doormat. He'd said she could have anything she wanted to make her happy. What would he say if she told him she wanted to go back to modeling after the baby was born? What would he say if she said *that* would make her happy?

He said nothing.

Dimitri stared at her across the width of the bed, his blue eyes unreadable, his naked body erect and for once not showing the least signs of desire. Waves of something feral rolled off him and made her shiver.

"Do you have a problem with me returning to my career after the baby is born?"

His hands fisted at his sides and his jaw clenched. "In New York, you told me you didn't want to return to modeling."

She shrugged. "I didn't think I had a choice. The life of a single parent is difficult enough without pursuing a career as demanding as that of a model."

"You want to leave our son to be raised by a nanny?" Distaste tainted every word he bit out.

No. Damn it. That was not what she wanted. One of the things she'd been looking forward to after her marriage was the ability to stay home with her baby. She wanted to breastfeed. She wanted to be there for her baby's first word, his first step. What had her muddled thinking that morning led her to?

"I don't have to take every assignment. I can give up catwalks and commercials and concentrate on photo shoots."

"You can give up your job entirely." He glared at her. "You are my wife. *You have no need to work.*"

She gripped the sheet covering her until there was a

bunched up wad of polished cotton in her fist. "Are you saying you refuse to let me?"

He rubbed his eyes, looking as tired as he had that first day in New York. "Would you listen to me if I did?"

"I'm going to live my own life, if that's what you mean."

"When have you ever done anything else?" He climbed into bed and turned out the light before lying on his side facing away from her.

Evidently the discussion was over.

She scooted down and turned on her side, trying to get comfortable. She'd grown used to the security of Dimitri's arms around her while she slept. Now, the width of the king size bed divided them. She felt stupid tears burn the back of her eyes. She'd brought this on herself.

She didn't really want to go back to modeling. It had only ever been something she did to provide for her family. Something she *could* do with the resources at her disposal. Now, she'd threatened to return to it for nothing more than to anger Dimitri just because he didn't love her.

Okay...maybe not just to make him mad. A small part of her had hoped, against all evidence to the contrary, that he could accept her for what she was, not what he wanted her to be. She had thrown down the gauntlet of her career as a test, she realized now. A test that had failed spectacularly.

She had been looking for a way to assuage her feelings of rejection suffered as Xandra Fortune, his lover. Stupid. She'd only opened herself up for more of the same. Hot tears leaked out between her tightly shut eyelids and she sniffed, trying to swallow back the tears and pain.

Sudden heat engulfed her and she was surrounded by hard, masculine muscle. "Do not cry, *pethi mou*. I am an idiot. If you want to pursue your career, I will not stand in your way."

"Dimitri?"

"Who else?" he asked with lazy humor as he tucked her into the curve of his body.

That wasn't what she'd meant. "I knew it was you...I'm just surprised at what you are saying." She wished the lights were on so she could see his expression. Did he mean it?

"I am accustomed to getting my own way."

She gave a watery smile he couldn't see. "I know."

"I am sometimes arrogant."

She didn't answer, thinking silence more politic than speech.

"I hated the time your career took away from me before, but I must not be selfish. If it is what you need for happiness, I will not stand in your way."

Had he really hated to be away from her? "It won't embarrass you to have a model for a wife?" she probed.

"Why should it? I was not ashamed when you were my lover."

"That was different. You even said so."

"I said many things I learned to regret," he said heavily.

"Mama would have a hissy fit."

"I will deal with your mother. She thinks I am a god, I have returned to her the family home."

The remnants of Alexandra's tears turned to laughter. "You mean it?"

"Yes."

"Turn on the light," she pleaded.

"Why?"

"I want to see you."

He humored her and a second later the soft glow of the bedside lamp illuminated his chiseled features. Sincerity burned in his eyes.

"You really will support me returning to my Xandra Fortune career."

"No." His mouth set in a firm line.

She sucked in her breath on a wave of pain. She'd been mistaken. He couldn't accept the woman she'd been.

"You can model, but you are Alexandra Petronides. You will not deny me my place in your life."

The arrogant statement should have infuriated her, but instead it made her heart sing. Not only would he support her career as a model, but he had no desire to distance himself from it by her using a working name.

He didn't love her, but he did respect her. "I don't want to be a model," she admitted.

His expression turned to stone. "What?"

"I want to stay home with the baby."

"Then what the hell has this last half hour been about?" he demanded in a shout that hurt her eardrums.

"Don't raise your voice to me!"

His jaw clenched and she could just see him counting to ten. "Why did you tell me you wanted to be a model when you did not?" he asked, teeth gritted, eyes spitting frustrated anger.

"I needed to know."

"What did you need to know?"

"If you accepted the woman I was…the woman who became pregnant with your baby. When you asked me to marry you, I was living as Alexandra Dupree."

"They are the same woman. I have said this before."

But she hadn't taken it in, or maybe she hadn't believed him. "You tossed me out as Xandra Fortune."

"You thought if you went back to modeling and calling yourself this other name, I would do so again?" he asked, outrage lacing every syllable.

"No, of course not." But it all seemed muddled now. None of her thinking since discovering his second promise had been particularly clear. "I don't know."

He flopped back on his pillow and covered his eyes with his forearm. "You are never going to forget, are you?"

"What do you mean?" she asked anxiously.

"My stupidity. You will never trust me enough to let yourself love me again."

"You don't believe in love," she reminded him.

He moved his arm and she flinched at his bleak expression. "You do not know what I believe in, Alexandra."

"Why didn't you tell me about the second promise to your grandfather?" she asked in a whisper. She hadn't meant to ask, but now that the words were out, they could not be unsaid.

He sat up, his body vibrating with something she would not label defeat in a million years. "This is why you put me through hell tonight thinking you wanted to go back to a career that always came before me?"

"It didn't come before you."

"*Ohi?* No? *I can't come with you, I've got a photo shoot. I'll be gone for a week to do the commercial. We can't make love right now, I need to sleep so I won't look like a hag in the morning.*" He repeated excuses she'd given him in the past with cruel sarcasm. "Even our damned sex life was dictated by your career. Do not say you did not put it before me.''

"I had to work, Dimitri. You know why now.''

"But I did not then and you did not enlighten me.''

"I couldn't.''

"Why not? Why could you not tell me who you really were?''

"Because…''

"I will tell you why. You did not trust me. You gave me your body, but not your trust. Not your heart.'' His Greek accent had gotten very thick.

"That's not true! I loved you!''

He slammed out of bed and towered over it on the opposite side. "Such a love I can do without. You lied to me every day we were together.''

She gasped in outrage. "I did not lie to you.''

"You said you were Xandra Fortune.''

"I was Xandra Fortune.''

He sliced through the air with his hand. "What is the use? You rewrite history to suit your own purpose.''

"I don't have to rewrite history to know you kicked me out of your life like a pile of garbage!'' she screamed at him, shocked at her own loss of control.

His shoulders slumped, his face looked haggard. "It will always come back to this, will it not?'' He turned away.

And suddenly she was out of bed, vibrating with rage suppressed for months while pain and despair held sway. "Don't you turn your back on me, you bastard!''

He spun around. "What did you call me?''

"Nothing worse than what you called me that day at *Chez Renée*,'' she accused.

"I called you nothing that day.''

"You called me a whore!''

He looked shocked. "I did not say this."

"Yes you did. That damn jeweler's box said it for you!"

"I bought the bracelet before my grandfather's heart attack. I had meant it as a gift to express my affection...then in my jealousy it became something else."

So, it had been a bracelet. She'd never looked. "You expect me to believe that, after what you said that day?"

"No." He shook his head. "I do not expect you to believe anything I say. You did not trust me before I betrayed our love, how can you possibly trust me now?"

In the red mists of fury surrounding her, she doubted her hearing, but she could have sworn he'd said he'd betrayed their *love*. She shook her head, trying to clear it.

"As I thought." He stood there in silence for several seconds. "Is there anything more you wish to say?"

She slowly jerked her head to one side in a negative. She'd said enough.

He braced himself, as if for a blow and then nodded. "I cannot sleep here tonight next to a woman who hates me. I cannot hold you in my arms knowing you suffer my touch for the sake of our son."

She felt her heart contract like a vise had been clamped onto it and was being slowly tightened. "I don't hate you." As for suffering his touch, how could he think that?

His eyes said he did not believe her.

He went into the dressing room and came out wearing a robe. "I'll sleep next door in the guest room."

She wanted to beg him not to go, but her tongue would not form the words. His hand was on the door handle when she asked, "Why didn't you tell me about the second promise?"

"I knew you would believe I had only come after you to keep it. I needed you to believe I wanted you for myself." Then he opened the door and was gone.

I needed you to believe I wanted you for myself. You never trusted me. You lied to me. You hate me. Dimitri's words ran like an unending refrain through her head. *Such a love I can do without.*

Love. He had said he had betrayed their *love*. She knew it. While she'd been screaming her invective at him, he'd admitted he had loved her. Did he still love her? Could he after the way she'd rejected him over and over again since he found her in New York?

She still loved *him*.

She did love him, but she hadn't acted like it. Not when they'd been together in Paris and not since his resurgence in her life. She had withheld her secrets, herself and her trust. What kind of love was that?

The only kind of love she'd known—conditional and with limits. Her limits had been born of fear, but they had damaged Dimitri as much as her mother's limits had hurt her. Alexandra felt that knowledge clear to her soul. She had wanted to receive unconditional love, but she hadn't been willing to give it. Was it too late?

She went toward the dressing room with one purpose in mind. She flipped on the light and started sifting through her lingerie. There had to be something, then she remembered and started looking for white gossamer. Dimitri had bought it for her their second week together. It was a flowing nightgown with a princess cut and yards and yards of gossamer fabric that fell from the gathered waistline below her breasts. The wide straps accentuated the delicate curve of her shoulders and it had reminded her of a wedding dress…a see-through wedding dress.

It was one of the few gowns that would fit over her

pregnant stomach. She slipped it on, her mission firmly in her mind. To be on the safe side, she pulled a robe on over it as well. No telling who might be wandering around in the hall outside her door to witness her state of dress. Security cameras at the very least.

She sifted through her cosmetic bag until she found a hatpin she used to unstop clogged tubes of makeup. She walked over to Dimitri's dresser and pulled out the bottom drawer. The pregnancy test was still there. With it and the hatpin clutched firmly in her hands, she left the bedroom.

Dimitri had said he was going to be next door in the guestroom. The door to the room on the right of their bedroom suite stood open. The door to the left was closed. She walked toward it. She tried the handle. It turned in her hand and she breathed a sigh of relief. She hadn't had a grandfather with tremendous foresight see that she was taught how to pick a lock.

The hatpin was for effect.

She opened the door and stepped into the room. The bed was empty, she could see from the light spilling through the open doorway. There was no other light in the room. She didn't need light to know he was there, though. She could sense the presence of the other half of her soul as surely as she knew her feet were attached to her body though she couldn't see them.

He stood at the window, his hand gripping one of the heavy draperies. He'd shed the robe he had been wearing and the sculpted muscles of his virile body lured her with animal magnetism. She could never let this man go again.

"Go back to bed, Alexandra."

She dropped the dressing gown and took a step toward him. "Make me."

He tensed, but he did not turn around. "I am in no mood for further arguments. Spare us both more unpleasantness and leave me. Please."

CHAPTER THIRTEEN

It was the "please" that did it.

She couldn't stand to hear her proud Greek husband pleading with her.

She flew across the room and landed against his back, her arms going around him like channel locks. She felt the baby move and kick. She was plastered so close to Dimitri, he had to have felt their son as well.

His entire body shuddered as if he'd been touched by a live electric wire.

She pressed her face into back, kissing him with feverish intensity. "I don't hate you. I love you," she whispered fiercely against his skin. "I'm sorry I've expressed my love so dismally you can't believe me. Love is supposed to be generous, but I've been too busy protecting myself."

He forcefully peeled her hands from his body and spun around. "Don't *yineka mou*. I cannot stand it. It is I who have hurt you. I who stupidly rejected your gift of a child, your gift of yourself. You have nothing to reproach yourself for."

"Don't I?" She shook her head and placed her hand over his mouth when he opened it to speak. "Please. Let me say this."

His lips moved against her palm in a kiss as gentle as the brush of angel's wings and he nodded.

She lowered her hand and stepped back from him. She met the blue depths of his gaze and held it. "I love my mother, but she's always doled out her approval and af-

173

fection based on my performance as her daughter.'' Alexandra took a deep breath and let it out. ''I learned early on that love was conditional, that it had limits and that it hurt.''

He nodded as if he understood and considering his background, she had no doubt he did.

''So when I fell in love with you, I set limits on that love, impossible conditions you had no way of meeting. I didn't tell you the truth because I was afraid to. You were, you are, this incredible guy, Dimitri. You teased me about how my mom sees you as a god among men, but for me it's no joke. You're so much more than anything I ever believed I could have. More generous. More sexy. More wonderful. More man. More everything and I couldn't believe you wanted me.''

She sucked in more air, trying to control her emotions, before going on. ''It shocked me that you'd want Xandra Fortune, but I was sure you wouldn't want Alexandra Dupree, a convent educated girl from a conservative family that had lost all its money. And to be honest, I thought if I kept that part of myself from you, I could protect myself from you taking me over completely. There would still be that part of me left when you were gone.''

At his look of dawning understanding, she nodded. ''You were right in Paris. I did expect our relationship to end, though I didn't consciously acknowledge it at the time. By keeping the other part of my life from you, I was preparing to go on when it did. But it didn't work because as you've said more than once—I was both Xandra Fortune and Alexandra Dupree with you. I grieved your loss in my other life as surely as I would have grieved if I'd stayed in Paris.''

"I wish you had stayed. I would have found you sooner."

She grimaced. "I didn't think you wanted to find me."

Devastating pain radiated from his eyes. "I know. This is my fault."

She didn't deny it. They each had their portion of blame for the disastrous end to their relationship.

"I should have told you where I was going on my trips. I made it easy for you to distrust me and when I told you about the baby, it was understandable you thought at first I might have had a lover."

"No! It was not!" The words exploded from him. "I let my mother's behavior color how I saw *you*. I had no reason to distrust you. You were so generous with me when we made love, so giving of yourself. I knew, I *knew* you could not have been that way with anyone else, but I was fighting a rearguard action against ending up as obsessed as my father had been. The feelings I had for you made me vulnerable. That was not acceptable, so I acted like the bastard you called me."

Tears clogged her throat. "No."

"Yes. My only excuse is that I was not thinking clearly. Worry for my grandfather, frustration over the promise he had extracted from me, it played hell with my thinking processes. The worst part was the desperation I felt at the thought of losing you. It horrified me and when I am afraid, I act. I lashed out at you and I lost you."

"I waited a week for you," she said helplessly. Not wanting him to feel worse than he already did, but wanting him to know she'd loved him enough to stay even after he had her evicted from the apartment. "I didn't leave until I saw the announcement of your engagement to Phoebe.''

His eyes closed and his head went back, his jaw taut. ''I knew I'd made the biggest mistake of my life when I let my grandfather put the announcement in the paper. It all hit me. How wrong everything was. How wrong everything would continue to be if I didn't get you back, but you were gone, *pethi mou*.''

There was a wealth of pain in those words.

''I'm sorry,'' she whispered.

''I could not find you,'' he said, as if she hadn't spoken, ''I had my detectives looking everywhere, but you had disappeared as if you didn't even exist. When I slept, I had nightmares of you falling down a deep hole and vanishing forever.''

His skin broke out in sweat at the memory.

She stepped forward and laid her hand against his heart. ''Losing you hurt so much, I thought I was going to die.''

He crushed her to him. ''I'm sorry.''

Two words sincerely spoken, words she had never heard him say in all the time they had known each other. And they healed wounds deep in her heart.

''I love you, *mon cher*.''

He kissed her with a passion that seared her soul. She was lost in the beauty of his kiss when he pulled away abruptly.

''Ouch.''

She looked up, dazed. ''What?''

''Something poked me.''

She looked down at her left hand where the hatpin protruded from her tightly clutched fingers. She lifted her hand and opened it to reveal the two objects she held. ''I think it was the hatpin.''

"Hatpin?" he asked as if he didn't know what one was. Maybe he didn't. Not many women had them anymore, but her mother was old fashioned. She still carried starched hankies.

"Yes."

"You planned to wear a hat?"

She laughed softly. "No. It was to pick the lock."

"But I did not lock the door."

"I wanted to be prepared."

"You know how to pick a lock?" he asked, a smile tugging at his mouth.

She shook her head. "I wasn't going to let that stop me."

He laughed and pulled her back into his arms, this time with more caution. "Alexandra Petronides, you are my dearest treasure and I will love you forever."

She gulped back tears and pleaded, "Say it again."

He cupped her face between the solid warmth of his hands. "I love you whether you are the independent career woman, Xandra Fortune, the spitting kitten, Alexandra Dupree or any other persona you choose to take on. You are the wife of my heart."

"Show me, Dimitri."

And he did. Beautifully. Erotically. Thoroughly. Then he carried her back to their bed and showed her again. She fell asleep in his arms.

"So, what was the pregnancy test for, *agapi mou?*"

Dimitri had convinced Alexandra to redon the shimmery nightgown from the night before and she sat curled in his lap in a chair on their private terrace a little after sunrise.

"Just a minute. Let me show you." She jumped off his lap and went in search of the small white stick. She found it with the hatpin on the floor of the guestroom. She went back out onto the terrace and couldn't help smiling at the picture her husband presented in nothing but a pair of black silk boxers.

Her gown covered more of her body with fabric, but none of it with modesty and his eyes gleamed their appreciation at her as she approached him.

She knelt down on the tile by his knees and presented the pregnancy test to him. "I'm pregnant with your baby, Dimitri."

His eyes widened, then narrowed in understanding. "You are giving me a second chance."

"Love can erase the mistakes of the past."

Something profound moved across his features and he reached for the stick. "I can think of nothing greater in life than to have you carry my child."

They were the words she had wanted to hear so much five months ago and she smiled with a radiance she made no effort to hide. "I love you, *mon cher.*"

She'd said it so many times over the past hours, the words should have lost their impact, but she knew they never would and the expression on his face told her he felt the same.

"I love you, Alexandra. Never leave me again."

"Never," she agreed fervently.

He leaned down and kissed her softly before lifting her back into his lap.

"I still feel bad about your grandfather," she admitted.

"Why should you feel this?"

"All those awful news stories. They must have devastated him."

Dimitri tilted her chin so they were looking into one another's eyes. "It was not the tabloid gossip that upset

Grandfather so badly he had another attack.'' Guilt chased across Dimitri's features. "I am fully to blame.''

"But…''

"Grandfather didn't even see the news stories until after coming out of the hospital.''

"I don't understand.''

"I told my grandfather I couldn't marry Phoebe and then I told him why.''

"Because I was pregnant with your baby.''

He shook his head, his eyes warming her. "Because I love you. He had the heart attack when he started yelling at me for being a fool after I admitted I'd evicted you from the apartment and could not find you.''

She couldn't take it in. "You already knew you weren't going to marry Phoebe before the tabloids ran the gossip about us?''

"I knew I wasn't going to marry Phoebe the day you told me you were pregnant, but I was insane with unreasonable jealousy, angry at myself, angry at my grandfather. I went off the rails and didn't get back on them until I saw you standing next to your sister that first night in New York.''

"I don't know. You acted pretty derailed then too.''

"She told me you had died! Do you have any idea what that did to me?''

She was beginning to have an inkling. If he had loved her, and now she knew he had, such news would have been soul destroying. "I'm sorry, Dimitri.'' She leaned forward and kissed him, wanting to heal the hurts of the past.

He kissed her back with enough passion to leave her gasping for breath a minute later.

"I don't know if I can ever forgive myself for what I did to you.''

Her eyes misted, but she smiled. "Please. You have to. I don't want to spend the rest of my life looking back. My present is glorious now that you are in it, now that I know you love me!"

"I saw the paparazzi outside the restaurant in New York and did nothing," he said with the air of a man who felt he had to admit everything.

She tried to figure out what he was saying. "Are you saying you wanted them to make the connection with my Xandra Fortune identity?"

He did his best to look humble, but it didn't come naturally. "I realize this was wrong."

"But you would do it again."

"I was desperate," he defended.

Dimitri desperate. Her heart just melted. "That's really sweet, *mon cher*."

"You are not angry with me?" he asked warily.

She snuggled closer, curling her fingers in his chest hair. "No. It's flattering to think of my Greek tycoon so desperate he stooped to nefarious means to win me," she said cheekily.

"I will never let you go again," he growled against her temple and then did something truly amazing with his tongue to her ear.

She shivered with the excitement only he could generate. "You're stuck with me for life, Dimitri Petronides."

"Count on it, *agapi mou*."

The baby kicked and they both laughed.

She rubbed the taut skin over the protruding little foot. "He approves."

"He's already brilliant," said the proud papa.

"Mmm…" she agreed, feeling contentment clear to her toes.

Dimitri shifted under her and she felt another protruding member, but this wasn't infantile at all.

"You look very sexy in that nightgown, even more sexy than you did when I first bought it."

"Over six months pregnant and you think I'm sexier than I was when we first met?" she mocked, secretly thrilled by the compliment.

He didn't smile at her joke. "Yes. Sexier. More beautiful. More everything because now you are mine and I know you are mine."

"For the rest of my life," she affirmed.

And then she set about showing him the kind of love she planned to give him for all that time: a passionate, unconditional, without limits kind of love.

Dimitri stood in the doorway of the Dupree Mansion nursery watching his wife tuck their small son into his cot. Little Theo, named after his great-grandfather, was nine months old. He had loved the excitement of Christmas, but had been ready for bed a good hour before Alexandra had been able to prize him from his fond grandmother's arms.

Cecelia had been in her element hosting Christmas for her family and Dimitri's besides in her New Orleans home. Alexandra had asked him to let her mother do it and as with so many things related to his wife's desires, he hadn't even considered saying no. She was the love of his life and he would do anything to make her happy.

He'd learned to appreciate the difference between that and the obsessive love his father had suffered from toward his mother. Alexandra had shown him by wanting only the best for him in return. It was a heady sensation.

Alexandra laid her hand on Theo's back and sang a soft French lullaby. Far from letting a nanny raise their son, she had insisted on seeing to all his needs, including midnight feedings, three-in-the-morning feedings and dawn wake-up calls to change Little Theo's nappy for the first few months. Dimitri hadn't minded. He liked getting up with Alexandra and watching his son nurse. It was a sight so beautiful, it transfixed him.

She was an amazing mother and an even more incredible wife. He thanked God daily for second chances.

She finally felt all was well with their son and turned to leave the nursery. She smiled up at him, her face soft with love. It was a look he would never take for granted again.

"He's out for the count."

Dimitri put his arm around her and drew her next door to their bedroom. "I have something for you."

"Dimitri." She drew his name out like it had six syllables. "You've already given me a mountain of gifts today. It's worse than last year."

He smiled in remembrance of their first Christmas together. They'd spent it with his grandfather in Greece. She'd cried when he gave her an eternity ring. He'd almost died from pleasure when she gave him his gift later that night…herself wrapped in a see-through red nightgown that had made her look like a very sexy, but pregnant elf.

Her eyes were soft with a love. "You're spoiling me."

"It is impossible to spoil perfection."

She shook her head. "I'm far from perfect."

She always said things like that, as if she wanted to remind him she was flawed and he always reminded her he would love her forever regardless. Which he did again and she smiled her contentment and love back at him.

They reached the bedroom and he pulled her to sit on

the edge of the antique four-poster. Then he pulled a small gift wrapped in red foil and topped with a tiny gold bow from his pocket. "Happy Christmas, *agapi mou*."

With a smile on her beautiful lips, she carefully tore the paper from the white jeweler"s case.

She remembered it.

He could tell because just for a second, she looked uncertain and then her eyes glowed undying love at him. Her fingers trembled a little as she opened it, then she gasped.

He withdrew the bracelet from the box and attached it to her wrist. When he looked in her beautiful golden eyes, she was crying. "Are you all right, *yineka mou?*"

She nodded, but had to swallow before she spoke. "Is it the same bracelet?"

"Yes."

"If I had opened this, I would never have left Paris. It would have taken a crane to get me out of the apartment."

She understood. He breathed a sigh of relief. Finally this last ghost laid to rest.

The bracelet sparkled on her wrist, the intertwined hearts studded with diamonds glistening in the light.

It was not the parting gift of a man to his mistress. It was not even merely a gift of affection from one lover to another. The bracelet bespoke a deeper emotion than he had been willing to acknowledge or verbalize at the time, but she understood.

"You loved me then."

"I loved you from the morning after I made you mine. You smiled so sweetly, offering no recriminations to me for seducing you from your innocence."

"It took me a while to realize it," she said ruefully.

"I as well, but I will never forget it," he vowed.

"And you always keep your promises," she said, laughing like the teasing little torment she was, "just ask your grandfather."

"When they mean loving you, I do."

She went serious and looked at the bracelet again. "I wish I'd opened the box."

"I made you too angry to do so. I think I did it on purpose."

"Because you knew the message the bracelet would give me and you weren't ready to admit it then."

"I love you, *agapi mou.*"

She accepted his words without reproach. "I love you, *mon cher.*"

He pulled her into his arms. "Always."

She hugged him as if she would never let go and he knew she wouldn't. "Always."

And his mind spoke the words she did not say, but had proven over and over again she meant…love without limitations or conditions. His body spoke the message back to her and her smile was a benediction.

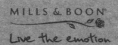

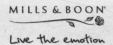

FREE

4 BOOKS
AND A SURPRISE GIFT!

We would like to take this opportunity to thank you for reading this Mills & Boon® book by offering you the chance to take FOUR more specially selected titles from the Modern Romance™ series absolutely FREE! We're also making this offer to introduce you to the benefits of the Reader Service™ —

- ★ FREE home delivery
- ★ FREE monthly Newsletter
- ★ FREE gifts and competitions
- ★ Exclusive Reader Service discount
- ★ Books available before they're in the shops

Accepting these FREE books and gift places you under no obligation to buy; you may cancel at any time, even after receiving your free shipment. Simply complete your details below and return the entire page to the address below. *You don't even need a stamp!*

YES! Please send me 4 free Modern Romance™ books and a surprise gift. I understand that unless you hear from me, I will receive 6 superb new titles every month for just £2.60 each, postage and packing free. I am under no obligation to purchase any books and may cancel my subscription at any time. The free books and gift will be mine to keep in any case.

P3ZED

Ms/Mrs/Miss/Mr ....Initials ....

BLOCK CAPITALS PLEASE

Surname ....

Address ....

....

....Postcode ....

Send this whole page to:
UK: FREEPOST CN81, Croydon, CR9 3WZ
EIRE: PO Box 4546, Kilcock, County Kildare (stamp required)

Offer valid in UK and Eire only and not available to current Reader Service subscribers to this series. We reserve the right to refuse an application and applicants must be aged 18 years or over. Only one application per household. Terms and prices subject to change without notice. Offer expires 31st March 2004. As a result of this application, you may receive offers from Harlequin Mills & Boon and other carefully selected companies. If you would prefer not to share in this opportunity please write to The Data Manager at the address above.

Mills & Boon® is a registered trademark owned by Harlequin Mills & Boon Limited.
Modern Romance™ is being used as a trademark.